WHEN MUSIC MEETS MURDER

Carli Cano Mystery Series

Book 1

Maryse Laflamme

• • • ●•●●• •

DEDICATION

As always, to Paul-Henri and Alexanne, my constant north stars, and to Olivia, the fiercest girl of all!

CONTENTS

UNLOCK CARLI CANO'S EXCLUSIVE PREQUEL—ABSOLUTELY FREE!

E ver wondered why Carli ditched the Big Apple for the colorful streets of San Miguel and a fashion wonderland of her own making?

The answer is juicier than you think!

Sign up for my VIP mailing list and get exclusive access to the **prequel that spills all the matcha tea** about it! This is one backstory you can only get here because it's NOT available elsewhere and never will be!

So, grab Your Free Prequel, *Stitched in Deceit*—Available Only to My Insider Tribe: https://MaryseLaflamme.com

Who needs a decoder ring when you can have the key to Carli's past? See you on the inside!

CHAPTER 1

I waited in line at El Café in Centro with Esme, my sixteen-year-old niece.

World music drowned out the surrounding private conversations, with relaxed people leaning toward one another as they repeated gossip and disclosed secrets they promised to never tell.

Once at the top of the line, we placed our orders, and the cashier handed Esme two small round cakes on sticks—cake pops. A chocolate one for me and strawberry for her, but she took a tiny bite of mine before handing it over with a grin. I glared at her, but she laughed. Typical Esme. I sighed.

"Anyone but you, *mi amor*, and whack! to the moon. You know that, right?" I flipped my right forearm and hand back and into the air on 'whack' as usual when I said this to anyone I loved who could get away with stuff around me.

Except this time, my hand hit something solid. Like brick solid. Like Manuel's chest solid.

"Manuel! Did you smell my chocolate cake from two blocks away, and come to take it from me, hmmm?" I gave him my best smile while knitting my brows together, but I dropped the fake anger pronto when I saw his face.

"What ... what's wrong?" I asked, my heart knocking hard in my chest, my whole body tightening up. A feeling from last night about something being off in my world rushed at me. I sensed it deep in my core, about an inch below my belly button—as if a twister was about to slam through my life.

Esme whipped her head around and, seeing the look on his face, frowned too. She stopped with the cake pop halfway to her open mouth.

Manuel looked, well, he looked ill, as if he were about to vomit. I hoped not; if he did that, he'd ruin the jewel buckle Manolo Blahnik pumps on my feet. Okay, okay, I know, selfish me. I stuffed that thought and took him by the arm and led him through the hissing of the coffee machine steamer, clinking cups and conversations all around us, around the corner in the back, through the door and onto the patio, Esme fast on our heels. The matcha tea I'd ordered would have to wait.

"What happened?" I asked. Please, *dio*, let nothing to have happened to anyone in our family. Please. My heart now seemed to want to burst right out of my chest, to explode.

His face tight, Manuel took a deep breath and dug deep into my eyes with his own. He shot a glance at Esme before answering.

"Millicent, Mil, she's, well ... she's dead." He shrugged, in slow motion, his eyes opened wide and resting on me as if I were the last thing they'd see.

I stared at him, my mind taking a moment to absorb the information. I waited patiently for him to tell me he'd made a joke, but his expression never changed. Besides, Manuel didn't joke about this sort of thing. He'd most likely seen too many dead bodies during his time as a detective in his pre-restaurant-owner days.

Still, he didn't know Mil that well, and didn't like her so much that he should be this upset, even if she really was dead. Did it have to do with her investment in his restaurant? How would her death affect that?

And this is what you're thinking now? I asked myself.

Also, to my discredit, a huge relief washed over me. Relief that it wasn't someone in our families. I ignored the confusion in my heart that said I should be more upset about Mil, rather than more relieved that nothing happened to my family.

Still, Manuel looked as if he'd been told that I'd died, for instance, rather than Mil. She was far north of 80 after all, and not in superb health, as far as I knew, and she wasn't most people's favorite. I nearly slapped a hand across my mouth for thinking such a nasty thought so soon after the poor woman's death. A death that did seem sudden.

Okay, I hadn't been too crazy about Mil's often harsh manner, and what Manuel told me about how she finagled her investment in his restaurant.

His passion for his restaurant was unmatched, but funding it hadn't been simple. He did not want to ask his father for the money. It would have been an insult—to not want to take over the management of the family hacienda as expected of him was one thing, but to ask for money for a separate venture?

So Mil's investment had been a lifesaver, but it came with its own pressures.

She expected comp meals for herself, always, and never failed to say, as loud as she could, "I own this restaurant, you know!" every time someone mentioned in her presence the restaurant into which Manuel had put all of himself without reservation—no pun intended. She meant it as a joke, but really?

I'd met her son, Liam, on several occasions. He lived in Dallas and visited often, a loving son. She had her circle of friends, other expats who'd moved here to San Miguel de Allende in Mexico, long ago, like her, and various social groups she belonged to. A full life!

And she'd never done anything to me, or anyone else that I was aware of, other than irritate us all with her way of flaunting her money, inserting herself into conversations without invitation, and her invasive way of asking about our lives. Private things. In public.

Enough, Carlota Maria Garcia Cano! I said to myself, using my full name as my mother did when displeased with me.

Now, tears stung my eyes. I mean, we'd seen Mil last night, had spent time with her.

"Are you sure? How?" I asked as thoughts of her raced through my mind.

Manuel nodded, then said, "Antonio came to tell me this morning, since I was at the party. They're looking at everything, of course, but right now, it looks like an overdose. Or possible poisoning. Which means ... well, it means the police wonder if she took, or was given, something that might have caused her death."

He said this with raised eyebrows, giving me that look, the one we used when we wanted to say something to the other without speaking. He glanced Esme's way, and I understood he didn't want to say anything about whatever this was in front of her

I frowned at him. Why the intensity? Why would that have anything to do with us, or anyone at the event? She hadn't died there. She'd left before we did.

And then, I thought ... if given something at the party, it might have taken some time to work through her system, *sí*?

Suddenly, dominoes fell over one another in my mind, as if clanging down on a table, clack, clack, clack, all in a row, little rectangular stricken soldiers.

Images from last night's party, where we'd both been, came rushing back to me. One stood out like a flare sent up from a sinking ship.

My eyes flew wide open like those of an old porcelain doll flipped upside down. My mouth dropped open, and my heart took a dive. All at once.

The noise of the bustling patio fell away.

"Oh, Manuel ... *mi querido* ..." No other words came to me.

We stood on the patio, staring at one another, not saying a thing. But, oh, how much communication transpired in those looks.

Esme's eyes toggled between us a few times. Then she gathered herself, shrugged, and said she was going to the restroom.

Now alone, I took Manuel's hand in mine and squeezed, the warmth of his palm seeping through mine. He took in a jagged breath, his grip tightening in response, his eyes meeting mine.

We stared at one another, both obviously stuck on the same image from last night.

Millicent was the primary investor in his restaurant. Because of what he'd done last night, even our cousin and friend, Antonio, San Miguel's *Sargento de Investigación*—the detective sergeant—would be forced to consider Manuel a suspect. If Mill had been killed.

Manuel and I, well, we have a history. I think I've loved him since we were infants. We'd been nursed side by side by our mothers, third cousins, which made us fourth cousins. They'd lolled away quiet afternoons in rocking chairs on the porches of their respective houses on our family's estate, Hacienda del Cielo Azul, the stillness only broken into by the occasional far away bleating of a goat, or roosters crowing, of cicadas in nearby trees. Ranch sounds. Our great-great grandfathers, brothers, had bought the land together, and it had connected our families since.

As the elder by three months, I'd always had an instinct to protect Manuel.

"Carli? What?" he said now.

My focus returned to him standing in front of me. "When will they know what she died of?" I asked.

Before he could answer, my mind wandered over to last night.

CHAPTER 2

The night before—when Millicent Jones was last seen alive—there had been an after-party at the home of my friends, Amy and Douglas, nestled in a development favored by many expats, a fifteen-minute drive from the town center. It offered a tranquility that contrasted sharply with the bustle of Zona Centro, the town's hub filled with restaurants and shops.

I'd wanted to arrive at the party *pronto*—before anyone else, or most anyone else. However, the tangled arteries of San Miguel's traffic, a testament to its rapid growth in too small an area, though great for business, kept my taxi at a frustrating crawl.

Still, I used the opportunity to do a quick check in my compact mirror; mascara, high cheek bones highlighted, nude lipstick, long, dark ponytail secured on the crown of my head. Done. I watched as we entered the lavish development of Los Frailles. Douglas and Amy's magnificent home waited at the end of a cobblestone street, its garden abuzz with excitement for the Música Clásica Esencial post-concert celebration.

Bougainvillea draped over walls, and rare trees and flowers sprouted in a cacophony of reds, oranges, pinks, greens, purples, and colors difficult to name, yet it felt peaceful.

Only good things could come of a gathering in such a lovely setting. All of me relaxed into the Zen-like atmosphere. I savored the privilege of partaking in an event with these lovers of classical music. A warm, engaging crowd. For the most part.

My anxiety-fueled aim in arriving at what my Mexican-side culture considered early—meaning at, or soon after, the time on the invitation—was to switch my place card so I'd end up sitting next to Manuel.

I mean, who knew who Amy had thought appropriate to seat me next to at dinner? Mischievously, she always did her best to put me—accidentally—in the company of men she thought would be a good match for me.

I waved at Millicent Jones, Mil to her friend, already meandering around the six round tables peppering the large lawn, six chairs at each. I watched her grab a glass of white wine from the tray of a passing server.

In true Mil fashion, she grimaced after her first sip. Seemingly, nothing ever pleased her. Yet, she kept the wine, and after spotting her name on a place card, she seated herself. Within the next thirty minutes, Música Clásica Esencial members would have all claimed their seats.

To my happy surprise, I found Manuel's and my place cards at the same table, one located behind Mil's. And more luck. Her chair was situated in such a way that she'd have to turn completely around to see me. I relaxed. I liked Mil, but in small doses. Many people felt the same, which had always made me sad for her.

I deposited my Mini Lady Dior Couture sequin bag in hot pink before my place card and took in the scene. In the rear of the property, a trio—harp, cello, and violin—quietly honed their instruments on a makeshift stage.

While Mil was preoccupied with a young man's greeting, I moved Manuel's name card from two seats down to the place on my right and put that place card where his had been. Satisfied, I looked around and noticed that from this location, we could see all the tables and the stage.

I made myself comfortable, but then thought I should go give Mil a hug after all since I'd now accomplished my goal. She meant no harm, just had a prickly personality.

Looking back now, I winced, realizing that I'd embraced her just hours before her death.

Before I could get up, though, a *muy guapo* figure of a man meandered into the garden. Dressed in a casual, yet classy Brunello Cucinelli suit that accentuated his muscular build, he was a vision of six-foot tall suaveness, my very handsome fourth cousin. His crisp white shirt was open at the collar, and his head sported dark, curling locks I'd tugged on, a lot, during our childhoods. Imagine a curly-haired Antonio Banderas, but even more handsome.

Manuel. His presence in my life ran much deeper than our family ties. From defending me against primary school bullies, consoling me when my cat, Calico, passed on my twelfth birthday, to protecting me from an unwanted suitor in high school, he'd been my rock. These were but a few of the countless times his support proved invaluable to me.

Also, he acted as my savior whenever I'd exhausted all my options and knew enough to seek help with something, except

I always let him think he was my first choice. Mexican male ego and all, you know?

Life without Manuel in it? No way.

He wove his way around the tables, looking around. Once I caught his eye, my whole being lit up like the Christmas tree at the Rockefeller Center in New York when first plugged in for the season. I smiled and pointed to his place card right next to mine on the table. He responded by giving me a thumbs up, and returning my smile with his own huge grin.

Manuel, a skilled flatterer—an important skill for a restaurant owner—always made time for Millicent, a patron and investor in his restaurant. The mastery of his charm, even towards vexing customers, intrigued me.

"Mil, Mil, Mil! So beautiful as always. You'll be breaking hearts tonight for sure."

As he spoke, he put his right hand over his heart like a silent movie actor expressing his love for a woman.

"Flatterer! I see through you, but I'll take my compliments where I can," Mil replied with a smile, checking the bouffant of her hair with her left hand, holding her wine in the right.

I smirked, amused, observing their banter.

I could only see her from the back, but could tell she raised her glass to take a sip. And ... there it was, as expected.

"Why the face, Mil? How's the wine?"

"Oh, it's a touch sweet for my liking. You know I prefer red, but as you can see, it hasn't been poured at this table yet," she explained, eyeing servers dispensing red wine two tables away.

The ensemble launched into a gentle Debussy piece—though lively Mozart or Beethoven might be better to keep the crowd alert. The melody muffled the ongoing conversation between Manuel and Mil.

The table to the left of Mil's from my vantage point already had one wine glass filled with red, just one, and both Mil and Manuel turned to look at it.

Now, seeing the scene with hindsight, I remembered ignoring a pang of foreboding as I traced their gaze. It might have been better if I'd paid attention to it and done something. But the friendly chatter of two of my mother's acquaintances now sitting two chairs away had distracted me from the goings-on at the next table. More people entered the garden with every minute.

Despite that, out of my peripheral vision, I saw Manuel walk to that next table and take the lone red glass of wine and bring it over to Mil. I glanced at him, and he winked at me. I winked back. It didn't matter that he'd "stolen" the wine—a server would be along soon to fill the other glasses at that table and would replace the one Manuel had just taken.

"Here you go, Mil, you heartbreaker, you!" I thought I heard Manuel say, handing her the glass. I could only make out portions of Mil's response, but understood enough.

"Ah, what a ... man you ..., my dear. *Muchos gracias*. Liam came ... town today to surprise me so I don't want to eat ... He said ... special dinner—he didn't ... about tonight ... So, only ... glass of red will hold me over," she replied.

Laughing out loud, she drained the rest of the white wine, put the glass down—and in one motion picked up the red. Oh, well. I hoped it worked for her.

They spoke for a minute more, then Manuel found his way to me. I stood to hug him, and we gave one another the obligatory cheek kisses. He looked me up and down in my Emilio Pucci wide-leg trousers in fuchsia, raspberry, tan, white, and black swirls, and silk Halston Heritage asymmetric neck tank top in raspberry.

"Carli, *te ves hermosa*," he said, each of his hands gently resting on my arms.

A small chill ran up my spine at the compliment that he found me beautiful. I should not be feeling that, I knew.

Once he settled himself, we conversed with the couple already at our table, and I paid little attention to Mil after that. Though her voice, like a distant waterfall, rose above the murmur of conversation, drawing attention to her table.

As guests streamed in, navigating to their tables and socializing, I saw many familiar faces.

These were my mother's acquaintances, not so much mine. My presence, like Manuel's, was due to concert tickets given to us by our mothers who'd extended their stay in Austin to care for an ailing aunt who lived there. When our mothers couldn't attend, they expected their children to do so in their place., though, this time, Manuel had missed the concert due to work.

The garden hummed with lively chatter as guests mingled and conversed, turning the music into a soft background melody.

Mil, engaged in animated discussions with her table companions, enjoyed frequent sips of wine. As her glass emptied, she gestured for a refill from a passing server.

She was clearly in her element amid the bustle. She wore her eighty-two years well. I saw most everything going on at her table, but, engaged in my own conversations, didn't pay much attention.

Because it happened on occasion, sometimes with a reason, sometimes with none, I'd ignored the sensation in the pit of my stomach, like that dizzying moment right before a roller coaster plunged.

Now, I realized that what I'd sensed had had to do with Mil.

And with the glass of red wine Manuel had handed her.

Why had that glass been waiting there with no one at the table and no other glasses filled?

More importantly, who had placed it there?

CHAPTER 3

A group of teenagers calling to one another as they took over the largest table, and Manuel's update on Mil's death, pulled me back to the present. His hand let go of mine, leaving behind its warmth.

"Not sure what she died of yet," he said, looking lost in thought. "No blood or sign of struggle. It looks like an overdose or poison. Maybe an aneurysm, but Antonio doesn't think so."

Something I couldn't put my finger on, though, could be seen in the depths of his eyes. He glanced at me as if gaging my feelings about the situation. His Adam's apple bobbed up and down, while the fingers of his right hand twitched as if he were trying to shake something off them. This confirmed his distress to me, a habit he'd had for as long as I could recall.

I felt a pang in my chest, recognizing his unspoken fear. In his eyes, I could see a hundred questions and what-ifs swirling around.

Without substantial evidence, a prosecutor might seize even the smallest piece to secure a conviction and close a case. Could the fact that Manuel owed her money ... and that he'd handed her a glass of wine that might have killed her get a guilty verdict? Even our family connections might not be enough to save him.

If it was *was* murder, Mil's prominence in the community would thrust it into the spotlight, intensifying the scrutiny. Such an event could affect the decisions of expats to settle here and affect tourism, both of which would hurt the town. Who wanted to visit, or settle in, a place where innocents like Mil were killed?

Our eyes locked, my heart thumping so loud I almost missed Esme's return and question.

"Wait! Who's Millicent Jones and why would someone poison her?" She half-whispered, her eyebrows reaching for her hairline, neck shoved forward, mouth forming an O.

Manuel and I shuffled a bit, then turned to face her.

He spoke first. "She's an elderly member of Música Clásica Esencial. We saw her just last night ..."

Her head moved between Manuel and me like someone watching a tennis match. When we said nothing, she continued.

"Why are you two so upset about her dying? Old people die every day, *sí*?" she asked, like any sixteen-year-old who, because of the size of our family, had attended more funerals than the number of years she'd been alive.

"You're right, *mi amor*," I answered her. "It's just that, like Manuel said, we saw her at a party last night, so it's odd to hear she's dead. She was having a great time, and now ... she's gone." I snapped my fingers while a lump formed in my throat.

Her eyes traveled between Manuel and me, her expression thoughtful but detached. "What does this mean for you two?" she finally asked. "Are you going to be involved in the investigation somehow?"

Just then a couple entered the patio from inside the café, two large standard poodles, one blond, the other black, leashed by their sides. I'd never seen them, or the dogs before. They were either newly transplanted—people moved here all the time—or they'd driven in from San Antonio, or Austin, or even Dallas, for a vacation. Many people drove in rather than go through the hassle of flying with large pets.

At the same time, the self-proclaimed world-famous (she always said this with tongue firmly in cheek) Josie Jolson entered the large patio from the street entrance on the opposite side, her three chihuahuas in tow. The poodles and Josie's dogs all made to get to one another. The chihuahuas barked up a storm, but from a place of safety behind Josie's legs, while the poodles kept pulling on their leashes, letting out short, low growls, counteracted by wagging tails. We had to move out of their way.

"So sorry!" said the woman.

She and the man allowed the dogs to pull them toward Josie and her brood. The three of us watched for a moment, smiling, as all the dogs circled, sniffing one another.

Josie's dogs, as usual, were dressed in costumes. Today's looked like those worn by Buckingham Palace guards, including bearskin hats, though shorter than those seen on the guards, most likely so they wouldn't fall sideways off their small heads. Josie had once told me she had all their costumes custom-made. I often wondered about putting dogs in those getups, but they didn't seem to mind. And they looked so cute.

Josie waved at us and smiled, and we all waved back. She then began talking with the poodle owners, so we returned to our own conversation.

"Of course not, Esme, we're not involved in the investigation. Of course not." Why was I repeating myself? As if I needed convincing? I'd had my fill of investigating a murder while in New York. It was one of the reasons I'd left it and come back home.

I looked at Manuel to confirm.

"No," he said, "that's the prosecutor and Antonio's job. I'm not a detective anymore."

He gave me a pointed look before continuing. "And your *tía* Carli here? That's not her job either." He obviously remembered New York.

I looked away from him quickly, not wishing to dwell on the warning in his eyes.

Esme responded. "Oh ... well, I'm sorry you lost your friend ..." she said, looking at us both. I didn't correct her.

She had to leave to get back to my shop where she was working this morning, and we said our goodbyes.

I hung on to the small hope that Mil had died of an aneurysm, something natural, anything but the wine Manuel had handed her. Because then he'd become a strong suspect, and I, a witness. The very thought made my heart ache and my head spin.

My thoughts tangled in knots, spiraling into a dark abyss of worry and guilt.

Could Manuel really be implicated?

The question gnawed at me, refusing to let go. The weight of realization settled in, while a chill ran down my spine.

His eyes, those eyes I'd known and trusted all my life, were now clouded with something I couldn't define.

And I was forced to confront a terrifying truth: if I got involved, it wouldn't just be an investigation.

It would be a test of everything unspoken between us, a test that could shatter our lives.

CHAPTER 4

The very idea that Manuel had killed Mil seemed absurd. On the surface.

Yet, the fear gnawed at me, relentless and cold. Every glance at Manuel became a search for hidden guilt, every smile a mask. Because New York changed me. Trust had become slippery. Especially with men I used to believe incapable of harm. Like Manuel.

He'd been a detective for three years, showing tenacity and fierceness. The man who once helped track down a cartel thief now handcrafted mole so complex it made people cry. Including me. Yet, fierceness hadn't left him just because he'd traded in his gun for kitchen equipment. God help the man or woman who'd dare harm anyone he loved.

But . . . that undefinable look in his eyes at the café came back to me

Could he have done it? Could he have handed Mil that glass of wine—knowing what was in it?

His time as a detective would've taught him how to cover his tracks. How to hide motive. How to kill.

And the motive might have been money.

I knew Mil had invested in the restaurant. But how much? And on what terms? The questions pressed in, hot and fast, making me wonder how we'd never talked about it when we talked about everything else.

The thought stung.

I tried not to think about New York. I tried not to think about what might've happened if we'd lived there at the same time instead of me on my way out, he on his way in—me in the showroom by day, him in the kitchen, and both of us giving in to the heat between us by night.

A blush crawled up my neck. Stop, Carli. Not now. Our families would never allow it. It was best that I'd left when I did.

Luna's voice crept into my head—soft and certain, from a conversation on the veranda months ago, when the sun had spilled golden light across the hacienda.

"You've been much happier since you came back. You're more the Carli I've always known."

She'd been right. I'd returned to the home of my birth. And maybe, my truth.

But now that truth had a murder in the middle of it.

I refocused on the matter at hand. Murder had come to town.

And I had to face it. To save Manuel. Even if he'd done it . . .

With a business to run, time was scarce. But this—this mattered. If Manuel was involved, it would destroy more than his reputation. It could unravel our families. Undo everything I'd built since returning. It would break my heart—shatter it into so many millions of pieces that it might never be possible to reassemble it.

Yet, my chin rose in defiance to those who might try to stop me from solving this, including the man standing in front of me.

I'd done it before, after all.

Looking at Manuel, I behaved as though no one had weakened his birthday *piñata* so much that its secrets could spill with just one whack of the paddle by me.

"When will they know?" Because Manuel and I shared such a strong bond, he knew what I was asking.

"Not sure. Antonio said they might send the body to Querétaro for the autopsy."

"Ah..." I hesitated. He looked so lost, like the weight of it all had just sunk in. "Are you okay?"

His gaze flickered—some mix of grief and something harder to place. "I'll be fine," he said. But the edge in his voice made my stomach clench.

The thought of Mil being dissected nauseated me, but my memory of Manuel handing her that wine glass, coupled with the potential money issue between them, made me even more uneasy.

Something was off. Something he wasn't telling me.

And that glass of wine . . .

And the money . . .

How deep did this go?

CHAPTER 5

Manuel kissed me on the cheek, saying goodbye, and I did the same. We left the café, going in opposite directions.

I decided to go home to ponder the situation. To my house in town, on Privada Pila Seca, not the hacienda. I'd bought it because living in town made running my business easier.

After a long day at work, I felt grateful for the short walk home—less than ten minutes—rather than driving twelve miles, the last on the dirt ranch road that led to my parents' house from the main road. Ranch workers kept the road well-maintained, but a dirt road in the dark is still a dirt road in the dark. Plus, I enjoyed the independence and privacy of my own house.

As I made myself matcha tea, I realized I'd left the one I'd ordered at El Café behind. Me? Forget a cup of my favorite tea? Unheard of. That said more about my state of mind than anything else. The murder investigation was clearly taking its toll.

Wait. Was I investigating?

Just as I sat on the couch to enjoy my tea and give myself a moment to think, Dapper, my cat, jumped on the couch and curled up next to my thigh—such a sweetheart—which lifted my spirit. But then, almost right away, my phone vibrated and rang, dancing on the coffee table. I picked up, heart speeding up at the same time. Antonio's face, yes, that Antonio, Manuel's friend, his third cousin, my third cousin, my friend, too—and the police detective sergeant—was staring at me from my phone's display.

In which of those capacities was he calling?

I decided against answering the phone and sent a text message to say I'd call him back later. I needed to think before we spoke. Guilt came over me, but why?

No rule existed that said I must answer every time yet another cousin called, even Antonio, the third member of the Three Musketeers-like friendship, that he, Manuel, and I shared.

Normally, I'd have picked up the phone for him.

Had Manuel told him I'd been at the party, or was he working his way through the guest list? Either way, I needed to decide whether to tell him Manuel had handed Mil a glass of wine. My story must not compromise Manuel, but I also could not lie to Antonio.

While all this swirled around in my mind like clothes in a dryer, I stared at the blank wall in front of me. The thought that it was more than time for me to find some art to put on it intruded. But my mind returned to the fact that, for me, no matter what, protecting Manuel came first.

No matter what ... why had that crept in? Manuel wasn't a killer, for goodness's sake! No need to no-matter-what it, was there? I took a gulp of matcha and nearly spilled some in the process.

The phone rang again. I shivered. But just Esme this time. I picked up.

"*Hola* Esme." I forced a smile.

"*Hola* Carli," she said, her usual sunny demeanor warming me despite everything. The girl had been born happy.

"I have Maryanne here. She's offering two-fifty on those red slingback Jimmy Choos."

The faint beat of Latin world music played in the background. It seemed to please most everyone, or at least not annoy them. It reminded me I should be at the store, especially on a Friday, and not trying to figure out a murder that might not even be a murder.

Maryanne, a sweet soul, but an astute shopper, always looking for an even-steeper bargain. She bought from me regularly, but there was no discounting everything for her.

First off, the merchandise belonged to those who consigned it. And if I always discounted it, but still paid the full agreed-upon price to the consignors, I'd have to close my doors and move back into my parents' house.

Plus, who would ever mark down a pair of Jimmy Choo shoes? Please!

"Tell her I can't do it for those, that the consignor told me she won't discount. Too many people are going to want them. We both know that, so I don't even want to ask."

"Okay, I knew you'd say that, but I wanted to look like I tried. She's by the dressing rooms, and I have my back turned, but I can tell she's watching me," Esme whispered into the phone.

I heard a bit of a giggle in her voice. Esme delighted in the sometimes-cloak-and-dagger workings necessary to run a successful resale shop.

We ended our conversation, and I sank back into my couch, a down-filled Henredon consigned last year and bought by me. It enveloped me as if I were a child sinking into its mother's arms. Next to me, Dap purred away, perhaps having a pleasant cat dream.

Now. What might have happened to Mil? When would the results of the autopsy be ready? Had anyone else seen Manuel hand her the wine? The most important thing to be concerned about?

My cheeks flushed as a fleeting thought passed through my mind, like someone moving quickly through a room where not wanted. Manuel arriving early, spotting her place card, spiking the wine, placing it at that table. Then leaving to return later, as if he'd just arrived.

But how could he have known no one else would drink it? That she'd end up with a glass of white she didn't like in her hand? URGH, these thoughts would make me *loca*.

No way he'd done that. Right? It's just that ... I had no idea how much trouble, if any, Mil's actions caused to Manuel's bottom line. He'd shared next-to-nothing about it with me.

Had he been sparing me, or planning something all along? Surely, he wouldn't benefit financially from her death? She had a son so I doubted that her will would mention Manuel, no matter how much she liked him. No, if he'd felt compelled to kill her, it was wrapped in that loan. Unless there was something else I didn't know about.

I shook my head as if that would loosen these dreadful thoughts enough that they'd leave my mind, flotsam removing itself from the edge of a body of water and floating away. No, not my Manuel. Not that he was *my* Manuel.

Nevertheless, I made an executive decision. No one would harm him if I could help it.

The only solution was to find out as quickly as possible who might have wanted Millicent Jones dead.

If she'd died from something other than natural causes, that is. Which looked likely based on all the information now in my possession.

Something rose from deep within me, just a whisper: though scary, solving that murder in New York had been exciting ...

Antonio might be a cop now, and Manuel might have been one in the past, but the three of us learned our love of solving mysteries while still in *primaria*—grade school.

We'd often figured out who'd stolen whose lunch. Once, we even solved the mystery of who stole the answers to a test to give them out to the whole school! It had fascinated us all, and given us a taste for investigating, even up to this day. Antonio, after thinking for a while, chose to make a career out of it. And so had Manuel until the foodie bug had stung him so deeply, there was no possible recuperation.

My thoughts returned to Mil. Let's see. Well, no friends. What? Of course, she had friends, at least a few. Well, mostly acquaintances, I'd say. No sense denying the truth if her murder—if she'd been murdered—was to be solved.

She belonged to Música Clásica Esencial and socialized with the group at those events. According to my mother, though, her way of pushing herself into conversations, and hanging on to them like a dog with a good bone after a long time without one meant few people invited her into their homes or for lunches and dinners outside the music events.

Did her death have to do with the organization? That made no sense to me, though.

She also met with a writer's group once a week and made it a point to drop this into almost all conversations. No idea how much writing she did, but she had had nothing published, choosing to commiserate with other writers who refused the self-publishing route, and hung on to one day being picked up by an agent or publisher. But why would anyone in either of these groups want her dead?

Could it be for reasons I didn't yet know about? Could someone else have had a problem with her?

I'd heard a rumor from Lisa Martin, one of the community's biggest gossips, about a nasty conversation that had taken place at a restaurant on the Jardin, the main square.

Mil had apparently told the world that Janice Johnson, her ex-best friend, owed her money, lots of it, and wasn't paying it back. Mil had lent it to her to buy the house she'd been renting when her landlord asked her to move out so he could sell.

Janice loved the house, but she'd needed more cash for the purchase. So, Mil had stepped in for her best friend who had lost a ton of money in the 2008 real estate crash, but expected a large inheritance. It would have allowed her to pay Mil back in full and all at once. But the inheritance never happened.

Would Janice have killed Mil to avoid paying her back—and to avoid further mortification every time the two ran into one another? Had she lost friendships because of Mil's constant angry talk about the money she owed her?

Seemed far-fetched, but all those episodes of various crime shows on Netflix made me realize that the improbable happened more often than we realized. Plus, my closeness with Antonio and Manuel and the cop experiences they'd often shared with me over time added to this belief.

Of course, there was Mil's son. He seemed to like and love her, but did he? Wasn't it only her who spoke of their close relationship? He'd behaved like a respectful, loving son on the few occasions I'd seen them together, but was it just for show?

Wouldn't he benefit with her gone?

No more dropping out of his own life for yet one more impromptu trip to San Miguel to take Millicent to the hospital for yet another imagined health crisis. She wouldn't go with anyone else. Was it how she got him to visit? Would he have visited otherwise? I wondered about his financial situation.

All this thinking wasn't getting me nearer to the truth. I needed to talk to people. Now that I'd cleared my head a bit about the whole thing, the best place to start, of course, was with my second favorite male cousin. I could get information out of him. The trick would be to avoid him asking me too many questions about Manuel and the party.

It's not like he'd ask me straight out if I saw Manuel give Mil a glass of wine.

Unless he already knew about it.

Chapter 6

I didn't like keeping this from Antonio, with whom I was nearly as close as Manuel, the three of us always adventuring while growing up together on the hacienda. Yet, this was Manuel we were talking about. With luck, Antonio would tell me she'd had a heart attack.

I sighed, picked up my phone, looking at it somewhat as if it were a bomb, but called him back.

"*Hola* Antonio! *¿Qué pasa?*" I said, making sure to smile so he could hear it in my voice.

"Carli! *Muy bien*, very well."

He and I mostly spoke in English with one another, like Manuel and me. Though it had started as a way for us all to practice as children, it had remained our habit even after we became proficient. His mastery of English had certainly helped him get the promotion to detective sergeant.

Because of the size of the expat population in San Miguel, much of which didn't speak Spanish, even after living here for years, at least one person in authority on the force needed to speak English like a native.

While growing up, I'd spent summers and holidays with my bio-grandparents in Austin, mastering English early and well. In our family's business enterprises, fluency in English wasn't negotiable for potential executives. My father joked that a good part of our success depended on dealing with "those people up north," instead of referring to them as Americans.

Though now I wouldn't be joining the family business. Whenever this came to mind, my thoughts usually also went to the fact that since I wasn't interested, my parents hoped for a grandchild to one day take over what would have been my position, but having a child wasn't really a part of my plan either—which I had not told them yet. However, if allowed to marry Manuel ...

No. Never. A union between us would be an unforgivable offense, since our great-grandparents had decreed that there were to be no marriages between cousins, not even fourth cousins like Manuel and me, which made us barely related. We shared less than a half percent of DNA. This, in a country where even marriages between first cousins were legal. Breaking the rule would mean becoming alienated from our families. We'd be forced to leave San Miguel and our beloved businesses, starting anew without family contact. Such a loss would taint our love quickly.

Coming out of my flash reverie, I jumped back into my conversation with Antonio.

"What do you know about Millicent Jones?" I held my breath, equally anxious and eager for his response.

"Ah, not much yet. Manuel told you." He said, clearing his throat.

"Yes ... it's so weird. I was talking to her just last night. It's hard to think of her as gone."

"I know." It came out deadpan. This sort of thing happened a lot in his homicide detective world, so it muted his reactions.

"What was it? I mean, it was natural causes, right?" I asked, my heart fluttering, a butterfly taking off from a branch. The phone slipped a little in my now-sweaty palm.

"Well ... we don't know yet. Could maybe be. But it might be poison, or medication, that's what the medical examiner hinted at, but, hey! Don't repeat that! I'm just talking to people right now. To see what I can find out. Routine."

"Oh, of course. But what would I know?"

Silently, I prayed he didn't ask about Manuel and a certain glass of wine.

Dap, a rescue, black from head down to pure white paws, lifted his nose tip at me as if he sensed my fear. When I'd first seen him at the shelter, he'd reminded me of dapper men from the Roaring Twenties when they wore black suits with white, or white and black shoes. So, I'd named him Dapper, but called him Dap. I petted him absently, intent on Antonio.

"Not sure. Maybe something she said to you last night? Was anything different about her?"

"Not really. Nothing stands out. I mean, she was her usual pushy, tell-me-everything-right-now Mil."

Wait. Not nice of me to diss a dead woman.

"Oh ... sorry. I keep forgetting she's dead, even though that's what we're talking about. I shouldn't talk about her that way ..."

He sighed loudly. "Well, it's still true either way. It's why we can't help but wonder. We're aware she wasn't the most well-liked. And all those money dealings with unhappy people."

He paused. I paused. Was he thinking of Manuel, too?

"Anyway, she was at the table next to Manuel's and mine, so I saw her talking to many people who came and went from her table but couldn't make out their conversations after a while, you know, all the noise from everybody talking around us, and my own conversations."

"Hmm ..." mumbled Antonio.

"I heard her say she wanted to go home early because her son had come into town in the afternoon, surprising her. I don't think she could have gotten him a ticket last minute; the concert sold out weeks ago."

"You were sitting with him?"

We both knew he meant Manuel.

"That's what you got out of all this?" I huffed. "Yes," I admitted

He chuckled a little.

"What?" I asked.

"Nothing." He took a deep breath, as if to put himself back on track.

"Okay. Anything else? Nothing you can tell me?" He asked.

I gripped the phone a little tighter. Why was he asking?

"Like what? It was just the usual party talk," I said, cautious. And thankful he couldn't see the color of my cheeks right now, which felt like they were on fire.

"Who did you see talking to her? Either sitting at her table or people stopping by?"

Oh, no. How did I answer that without compromising Manuel?

Just then, the beep of call waiting came through the line.

"I have to take this call, it's the medical examiner. Alright, well ... if you remember anything, call me," he said.

"Of course. I promise. I want to know what happened. Mamá will want to know, too. I'm going to call her now and tell her, though I'm sure she already knows. The Cano family grapevine, right?"

He chuckled, but with little enthusiasm, having been a victim of it himself, like all of us.

"Oh, I missed his call. I need to call him back. *Adiós*."

"Wait! How long will it be for you to get the results back from the autopsy?"

But he'd already hung up. My heart raced at the thought of how close I'd been to having to answer his question about who had spoken to Mil last night.

The phone rang again. Manuel.

"Hey," I said in greeting, still shaky.

"*Hola* Carli. I thought I'd tell you that I ran into Isa from the medical examiner's office. She told me they're sending Mil's body to Querétaro for the autopsy."

"Why? Wait! You told me that already. Antonio too."

Had Antonio told me? No, he hadn't. My thoughts were getting tangled up in my head, much like bumper cars coming together, then apart.

"No. Before, I told you they *might* send the body there. Now, I'm telling you they did."

I glanced skyward in irritation. You might take a boy out of his cop career but could never take the cop out of the boy. His exactitude sometimes made me *loca*.

My heart sank. Must be serious if they were sending her there instead of handling it here.

"Well, alright. I just got off the phone with Antonio. He actually didn't say either way."

Then I remembered he'd had to get off the phone quickly.

A heavy silence filled the space between us. Yet, we both realized that people who'd most likely died of natural causes were most-often examined here, or not at all. Not sent to Querétaro.

"It might mean nothing, Carlita."

Why was he calling me Carlita? I wondered, gripped by the seriousness in his voice. He reserved that name for grave matters or when he was in a teasing mood. But there was no tease in his tone now; he meant business.

• • • ● ● • ● ● • • •

He never dared call me Carlota, the name given to me at birth by my mother, for no reason other than she liked it.

But Carlota was the name of the ill-fated empress to Mexico, Princess Charlotte of Belgium, known in Mexico as Carlota of Mexico, after Napoleon III had sent her husband, Archduke Maximilian of Austria, to Mexico to head a French intervention.

Charlotte had come with him. The thing had flopped, and Maximillian and Carlota had high-tailed it back to Europe, which is when Carlota had lost her mind.

Who wanted to be named after a woman who'd lost her mind, princess or not?

When, at age 12, I'd learned this story in school, I'd renamed myself Carli, and ruled that everyone call me that. It was then that Manuel began to call me Carlita whenever he wanted to say my full name without insulting me. So, he'd changed that one letter. Genius, no?

Manuel continued. "Also, it's going to take some time. There was a triple murder over there last night. Cartel. They'll do those first and get to Mil Jones when they can."

Naturally, they'd think cartel autopsies more important than one on an 82-year-old woman who might have died of natural causes. I crossed my fingers.

Manuel and I said goodbye and agreed he'd come over when we'd both finished our workday to share a glass of wine and talk.

From nowhere, a thought popped into my mind at the speed of a racing car coming around the corner on the Grand Prix circuit.

I'd been asking the wrong question!

I returned to the right question. Questions, rather.

Who, besides Manuel, might have placed that glass of wine there?

And *in front of whose place card*?

Knowing this might shed suspicion on someone other than Manuel. And then my heart sank.

If he wasn't guilty, wouldn't he have already brought that up? Unless he simply hadn't looked at the name on the place card?

CHAPTER 7

N ow, if the wine caused Mil's death, what had been in it? And if Manuel had nothing to do with it (please, *Dios mio*, no!) who put what in it?

And why?

Why had that lone glass been there at all, filled and waiting, when no others were at that table?

I shook my head. I hadn't said anything to Antonio, thank God. As far as I could tell, he didn't know about the wineglass. Unless someone else had seen the exchange—and told.

Who had been close enough to witness it? My focus had been on Mil and Manuel, the clink of glasses, their laughter. I hadn't paid attention to who might have been hovering nearby.

I tried to get up and pace, think things through, but Dap leapt into my lap before I could move. Warm, heavy, wise-eyed.

"What?" I asked him. He always knew when something rattled me.

Maybe it was time to stop obsessing over Manuel and think about who else might've wanted Mil dead. If, that is, she was murdered. That possibility hung in the air, as faint and persistent as last night's verbena candle.

Dap purred in my lap, a deep, resonant vibration that seemed to convey his doubts. But what did he know? He didn't have a Manuel to protect. He blinked up at me, his eyes wide and innocent, keeping his opinion to himself.

What about her son?

They seemed close. Loving, even. But I'd seen it before—sons who resented being controlled, even when cloaked in affection. And Mil? She wasn't subtle when it came to opinions. Or control. I frowned. He'd been strangely quiet last night. Gracious, polite. But reserved.

And Janice? The broken friendship, the unpaid loan, the inheritance that vanished like mist. I still needed to find out if Mil had confronted her again. Or threatened legal action.

Janice had planned to use a promised inheritance from her single, childless brother to pay it off, only to discover, upon his death, that his wealth was a mere wisp of a thing, like a faint scent that vanishes in the wind, and not at all what he'd promised.

I sighed, gloom surrounding me like a thick fog, a tangible sense of despair in the air. What some people felt forced to do—even to family—just to survive. I thought of my ferocious but loving family, thankful I'd never have to revert to such tactics. It both warmed my heart and saddened me for those not blessed in the same way.

Back to the wine. I needed to know who was *meant* to sit at that table. Was the poisoned glass actually meant for Mil? Or someone else?

Did Amy keep those party seating charts?

If so, I needed them.

The thought pulled me back from the edge of sleep. I blinked, startled at how far I'd drifted. Dap stretched against me.

One more thing for my list.

Call Amy.

And Mil's son? If I wanted to know more about him—what he was like, what he might've been hiding—who would I even ask?

CHAPTER 8

D espite Mil's death—or her probable murder—I had a business to run, and the next morning found me at my shop a full hour before opening at ten, the key turning with a satisfying click as I entered the still space.

Normally, I kept the door locked for my first fifteen to twenty minutes to make sure all was in place.

The soft hum of world music for background sound? Check.

The gentle flicker and sweet aroma of a gardenia candle, safely positioned near the register? Check.

Changing rooms empty and mirrors spotless? Check.

Bathroom candle glowing? Check.

Floor clear, racks in order, ceiling fans on, pillows fluffed? Check, check, check.

I rearranged a few racks, sorted out sizes, dusted a few shelves—Sofia was running late—and at ten sharp, I unlocked the door, welcoming in sunshine, chatter from the courtyard I shared with a jeweler, an art gallery, and a new coffee cart from which I could smell espresso, a nice addition.

I'd begged the couple running it to offer matcha, just to save myself the daily trek to El Café. Friends teased me about my obsession, but if I was going to be addicted to something, at least it was green and antioxidant-packed.

Not ten minutes after opening, the wind chime announced Lisa Martin—Música Clásica Esencial member and reigning queen of local gossip. Her lavender-heavy perfume hit the air before she did.

Lisa and her husband, the ever-patient John Sullivan, had spent most of the previous night at the table in question. I made a mental note—*ask about the seating.* But first, small talk.

We commiserated over Mil.

"It's a shame, but at least she left the planet on a good day for her. You know she liked nothing better than a great concert followed by a fun party, eh," said Lisa, her eyes sparkling.

She'd retired here from corporate life in Canada and now dabbled in Reiki and astrology—typical for our town, where artists and free spirits outnumbered accountants ten to one.

"How did you like the concert?" I asked to make conversation, the echo of the orchestra still in my ears.

"Oh, very good, as always, thanks to Misha's efforts, eh," she said, her voice rising in pleasure.

"I hardly saw you at the party—just flashes of purple as you twirled past our table," I teased.

She laughed, tossing her hand in the air. "You know me."

As she browsed, she added, "I'm meeting Denise for lunch. Didn't get to talk to her much at the party—she seemed a bit put out when they left."

"Why was she upset?" I asked casually, untangling necklaces on the jewelry tree.

Lisa glanced around, lowered her voice. "It's Bill. Not taking his medication again. She's struggling."

She hesitated, lips twitching as if trying to hold back something juicier.

I kept my face neutral. Let her fill the silence.

"She told me something the other night I can't repeat, but really..." Her voice trailed off like a fishing line with a hook dangling.

The music switched to a soft ballad by Julio Iglesias, gentle guitar sounds filling the space. The soft guitar contrasted sharply with Lisa's crackling energy.

She drew a sharp breath, reeling herself in. "Never mind. You don't want to hear my gossip."

Actually, I *did*. And I had a feeling I already had.

Something about what she said scratched at the back of my mind—an itch I couldn't quite reach. I wasn't sure what it meant, but I felt it meant something.

Was Denise's tension just about Bill and his medication? Or something more? Something to do with Mil? And what medication was that?

Just then, a man and a woman came in and I called out to them.

"*Hola*, welcome, feel free to browse! I'm here if you have questions."

"Thanks!" said the man in a cheerful voice.

"What does he take medication for?" I asked, only being polite, of course . . .

"Depression," she whispered, even though the couple was too far away to hear. She leaned even closer toward me, lips pursed and eyes big, as she said it.

This town loved secrets. People said "Don't tell anyone" like it meant "Tell everyone immediately, but whisper." I only trusted a handful of people. Family. Luna. A few friends.

And with family like mine? Who needed outsiders to stir drama? We had enough telenovela-worthy material of our own.

To avoid making Lisa suspicious, I had to change the subject. And suddenly, I remembered. "Lisa! I nearly forgot—I've got Ferragamo ballet flats in your size in the back! Your favorite."

Her face lit up. "Oh my, what color?"

"Red."

She squealed, tried them on, and left happy, headed off to meet Denise—with a new pair of shoes and perhaps a fresher piece of gossip on her tongue.

But that lingering itch was still there.

I should've asked who sat at the table with John and her. Another missed chance, but I couldn't let Lisa leave thinking that I had something up my sleeve.

The store stayed busy. At two, I locked up for *comida*.

Normally I'd use the quiet to sketch or sort inventory, but today?

Today, I couldn't stop wondering if someone in that crowd had seen something. Or worse—done something.

CHAPTER 9

S ince I couldn't concentrate, I trudged home and grabbed a light lunch—carrot and celery sticks with my home-made hummus. Dap paced beside me, tail twitching like I'd wronged him deeply.

"You can sit with me in a minute, Dapperoo, *mi amor*. I need to eat first."

He glared but made himself scarce.

I sat, chewing and thinking. Obviously, I didn't want it to be Manuel. So, it was time to get even more serious about digging deeper into my other suspects—like Liam.

I'd only seen him a few times. Once, we'd ended up at neigh-boring tables at Hank's. I was with friends, he with Mil. She'd kept him close, clearly wanting his full attention. We'd exchanged polite greetings, a firm professional handshake, nothing more. Still, something about the way he looked past everyone else—like none of it mattered—had struck me as cold. Or maybe just reserved. At the time, I couldn't tell.

Still, I knew more about him than you'd think, thanks to Mil's frequent bragging. She talked about him the way some people talk about their dogs—over-the-top, loyal, a little blind. Property developer in Dallas. Renovated high-end condos. Built one from the ground up. According to her, he was successful.

But real estate was unpredictable. What if he'd had a bad year or two?

Mil had mentioned a "slower quarter" once in casual conversation, dismissing it with a wave of her hand, but at Hank's, she'd looked briefly annoyed when Liam had left the table to take a call.

Mil was private about her net worth, but judging by the house, the designer bags, the investments around town, and the loan she gave Janice, it had to be substantial. And Liam—her only son and heir—might not have wanted to wait for nature to take its course. Especially if he'd tied up more money than he had trying to prove himself.

I grabbed my laptop and did a quick search. "Liam Jones, developer, Dallas." Two pages of solid, boring success. Glowing reviews. No red flags. Still, the success felt . . . curated. Maybe that's all online success was. A polished façade.

I sighed, pushed the laptop aside, and made room for Dap. He hopped up like he'd forgiven me and curled into my side, purring loud enough to vibrate the cushions.

I ran my hand over his silky coat, eyes unfocused, thoughts drifting.

Luna was better at this sort of thing than me. By day, she was a freelance web developer, but moonlighted as a white-hat hacker, leading a band of like-minded digital vigilantes. Their idea of fun? Breaking into websites and databases—not to cause harm, just to prove they could. Crazy, if you asked me. They usually reported the flaws they found, anonymously, so it was technically a good deed—just done in a twisted way. But she was in Mexico City on a big contract, and I didn't want to disturb her just for this.

So, who had wanted Millicent Jones dead?

So many suspects. So many motives.

But Liam stayed near the top. Not because I thought he was dangerous—but because he felt like someone keeping something under wraps.

Drawn to the kitchen by the kettle, I considered making matcha but opted to head to El Café instead.

It was nearly three on a Saturday. The likelihood of running into someone useful was high.

And I needed to call Amy—finally—about that seating chart! Because it could tell me who that wine glass had been really meant for.

CHAPTER 10

I ordered tea and a cake pop, why not, and stood near the pickup counter, surrounded by the familiar sounds of El Café—the low hum of chatter, the whoosh and hiss of the espresso machine, and the rustle of paper cups being filled.

I saw Liam come in and seat himself at the table closest to the order counter. He noticed me too, and we waved at one another. He wore a deep scowl and looked like he needed sleep. His skin was pallid, and his eyes had the redness and sadness of grief. He had the demeanor of someone who'd been dropped into a new reality without warning. Which I supposed he had.

I walked toward him, the sound of my footsteps echoing softly on the tiled floor.

"Liam, *hola* ... I'm so, so sorry about your mom."

"Hey, Carli. Thanks ... I'm still not sure what to think, to be honest. It feels unreal. I mean, I was just here two weeks ago; we had lunches, dinners ..."

He trailed off, his voice thinning into a whisper as if the memory caught in his throat. His eyes glazed over, and I caught a look of agony. For a moment, he seemed to be somewhere else, lost in a painful memory, before shaking himself back to the present.

I tried to read into his sadness, into the lines of fatigue and distress on his face. Could he really have killed his own mother?

Not a nice thought about a man who'd so recently lost someone he loved, and who looked so distraught about it.

"I know, I know. So sudden." I said, my voice sympathetic.

I glanced at the pickup counter and noticed my tea was ready. I signaled to him to wait a minute by raising my right index finger, then headed over to get it.

Liam got up from his table then and walked to the order counter. As I passed by him after getting my tea, he asked if I wanted to sit with him.

How could I refuse the man whose mother had just died? Only a not-very-nice person would refuse him at a time like this. He needed to talk. To someone, anyone. That's all.

"Sure, I'd love to," I said, doing my best to convey warmth.

For the next twenty minutes, I made small talk and reminisced about the man's mother with him. She'd never been my friend, but I still managed to tell him a few anecdotes about her that made him smile, though sadly.

All the while, I sipped my matcha, its earthy taste grounding me, and I wondered what he thought about how she'd died. But no way would I bring it up.

"Hey, I have to get back to my store. *Comida's* over," I said finally, smiling, the slight bitterness of the matcha lingering on my tongue.

"Of course," he said, clearing his throat, his voice raspy from stress. He stood to give me a goodbye hug.

"I'll let you know about the memorial service. I'll, well, I'll create a post on the San Miguel's Facebook page she followed. She'll be cremated. It's what she wanted. So, pictures, yeah, I need to get pictures together," he continued.

His eyes darted left and right as if he'd find photos floating about. His movements were erratic, those of a man drowning in a sea of confusing emotions. Every inch of him vibrated with tension, like a taut string on the verge of snapping.

I suppose if it were my parents, the pain and shock might make me act strange and fidgety too.

He encircled me in his arms for a quick hug. It made me realize that he'd lost weight since the last time I'd seen him on his previous visit. This hug was less substantial, and he felt fragile.

Could someone lose several pounds in a couple of days after the death of a loved one? His shirt smelled faintly of musky cologne mixed with sweat and anxiety.

Was there anything I might do to lessen his pain?

When I left, I ran into Janice on her way in. One of my suspects. No shortage of potential killers in my world today.

"Well, Carli. How are you?" She asked, her voice steady, yet her eyes glimmering with a sharp curiosity.

"Janice. Nice to see you," I lied. "I'm well, thank you. Just headed back to my store.

"Liam's in there," I added, pointing my thumb over my shoulder toward the interior of the coffee shop, watching her face, my whole being on guard.

"Oh," she said, craning her neck in that direction.

Her eyes, shadowed by the brim of her hat, seemed to harbor hidden thoughts, making them momentarily inscrutable. The distant murmur of cars and laughter of pedestrians gave an unsettling backdrop to our conversation.

If knowing she'd see Liam made her nervous, it didn't show. She'd be a bundle of nerves had she killed his mother, right? I observed her closely, but could find nothing unusual in her demeanor.

Two groups of tourists who called to each other from opposite sides of the street distracted us for a moment, their voices jovial and carrying in the open air.

She turned back toward me and let out a deep sigh.

"I can't believe she's gone. I really can't." She looked me in the eye, her own filled with tears.

Her perfume, a delicate floral scent, filled the space between us, contrasting sharply with her somber expression. She was a first-class liar, if she'd been the one to do away with Mil.

"Yes ... it's odd how quickly it happened," I replied.

A look came into Janice's eyes as though she held some of her own doubts about me. Her skepticism was palpable, creating a faint tension in the air.

"Well, I'm not so sure ... she was older, and her heart. There was fear of a clot too at some point. She didn't talk about it, but things weren't superb health wise, that's for sure," she said, her voice betraying a hint of nervousness.

"Oh. I didn't ... she had heart problems?"

Janice shifted her Coach tote bag in blue Signature denim—which she'd bought from my store—from her right to her left shoulder. The rustle of the fabric filled a brief silence.

She fiddled with one of the straps while pushing a strand of her mid-length hair behind her ear with her other hand, her movements precise and controlled.

"I think so. No, I'm sure. She never said anything to me about it even when I asked, but she visited a cardiologist in Dallas every time she went. That much I know. But, we ... we haven't spoken much in the last year ..." she trailed off.

Interesting information. Still, it didn't seem to have been her heart. Janice's words hung in the air between us, a heavy unspoken question.

"I heard she might have been poisoned, though."

"Poisoned?" Janice's eyes got large, her mouth opened, her brows furrowed, and she made as if to step back away from me but caught herself. The shock in her voice was almost tangible. She gripped the strap of her bag. Good actress, or genuine reaction?

"Hey ladies, nice to see you, but can we get past, maybe? We're in dire need of some java."

This from a man, one half of a couple, the woman and the man wearing huge smiles, both in identical Rastafari t-shirts that said "Roots, Rock, Reggae," and sporting matching dreadlocks.

Matchy matchy, such a fashion faux pas, the fashionista in me thought. Still, they smiled so big and gave out such an energy of happiness, I grinned back.

They both laughed, and the sound resonated down the covered walkway and into the open courtyard, mingling with the distant hum of traffic and the soft sounds of conversations going on at the tables in the courtyard.

"Of course, so sorry, I didn't notice we were blocking the doorway!" I said.

Janice and I stepped away from the courtyard entrance and onto the cobblestone sidewalk to finish our conversation. The transition was brief, just a few steps, but it shifted us from the semi-private space to the public street.

"What do you mean, poisoned?" Janice whispered, her eyes still huge.

The occasional sound of a car passing by, along with pedestrians dodging us, punctuated our conversation, and the hard, uneven surface beneath our feet added to the tension.

"Well, it's not for sure. Please don't say anything. We have to wait for the, hmm, well, the autopsy," I whispered back, aware of the contrast between our hushed voices and the more robust sounds around us.

She gazed at me, squinting a little, speculation rampant in her eyes. Her nervous energy charged the space around us.

She knew my connection to Manuel and Antonio, and their connection to the police department. This told her from where that information had come.

"An autopsy." She blanched, her voice flat and low, almost drowned out by a passing car.

Her eyes drifted to the left as if answers might be found down the street behind my shoulder. She sighed deeply, the sound carrying the weight of emotion and uncertainty.

I nodded my head, wishing I could give myself a good kick in the tresero—the behind—for bringing that up at all. The thought made me wince, both in mental and phantom physical pain.

She'd blab about this!

Unless.

Yes, unless she'd done it, in which case, she'd keep it to herself. I brightened a bit at that, feeling a sudden warmth in my cheeks as my heart raced with realization.

I just had to keep in touch with anyone in whom Janice might confide, and they'd be sure to tell me the gossip, all the while telling me not to repeat it, of course. That would be a great indicator of her guilt or innocence.

Sometimes, a mistake was no mistake.

"Anyway, let's keep it to ourselves, but I really have to get to the store. Esme's not coming in today." I said, glancing briefly down the cobblestone street as the normal afternoon bustle continued around us.

"Of course," she said, her voice carrying a hopeful tone. "I hope you have a great day with lots of sales!" She called out.

I'd already started to walk away, but I turned and smiled at her. Did she seem like she'd killed someone? No.

But, of course, anyone who had committed murder would want to appear as innocent as possible. They'd play the game well, wouldn't they? To avoid prison? I shivered at the thought of a woman like Janice in a Mexican prison.

Then, I saw that coming toward me from about twenty yards away was Manuel.

I'd never get to my shop at this rate ...

Chapter 11

M anuel's eyes sparkled with mischief when he spotted me. My heart leapt, and I answered his grin with a smile that stretched to the very edges of my face.

The world around us blurred while we each navigated the narrow sidewalk toward each other, sidestepping pedestrians, and occasionally veering into the street to avoid them.

Until we came face to face, we stayed in our own bubble, as if magnetized by one another.

Whenever we ran into each other in Centro, we frequently played this game. We exchanged hellos with a quick hug and a kiss on the cheek.

"Cousin," he said in greeting.

"*Primo*," I said.

Sometimes, it would be me who said Cousin, and he'd answer *Prima*. Another game we'd started as children running wild on the hacienda. By saying it in the two languages we knew, it had made us feel as if we'd had a secret.

We didn't get any further than that, though, because, just then, a car pulled up beside us, interrupting our play. It was Antonio, and his serious expression signaled that he had something important to say.

Was he coming to arrest Manuel?

Then, I realized he was driving his own car, a generic four-wheel-drive vehicle of some sort. Makes and models of cars always escaped me. This one—as ancient as Moses—babied by Antonio like the anxious, loving parent of an infant.

Manuel and I moved to stand by the open passenger-side window.

"Antonio!" Manuel greeted him.

"*Primo*!" Said Antonio, and we all laughed because he knew our game and sometimes teased us about it.

"*¿Qué tranza?*" Manuel asked.

Antonio glanced at me, then around the crowded sidewalk, before continuing in English. Whether he was driving his own car or a police cruiser, many people in town were familiar with him, so he adopted a hushed tone, making it clear that what he was about to say was meant for our ears only.

"Still no news," he said. "But we're looking at all possibilities. There's no way to know right now what it was."

He spoke with his sunglasses pulled down his nose, a serious look in his eyes scrolling between Manuel and me like a computer mouse being moved across a screen.

I raised my eyebrows at him in response.

"When do you think you'll know anything?" Manuel asked.

Anton_o tensed.

"Those guys, they get back to you when they get back to you. You know that. No sense to push," he continued.

"Ah ...' was all I could think of to say. Waiting would make us all loco. Heart attack, aneurysm, poison, overdose, accidental or otherwise, or something else? Come on, Universe, tell me, I screamed inside.

A car honked behind Antonio, so he moved his SUV a little to the side, but the narrow street allowed little maneuvering. The car passed him, a vibe of disapproval heavy in its wake.

"Well, I have to get back to work." I'd said this too many times in the past hour, as if I needed to talk myself into it. Wouldn't sitting on my couch, Dap on my lap, be more productive, what with having to prove Manuel innocent?

"Okay, go run your little business, Carli," Antonio said, and winked at me.

Even though I knew he mostly didn't mean it, it made me crazy that he was talking as if sending me off like a little girl to go play with her dolls.

"*¿Mande?* That *little* business makes me a good living!" I retorted.

My cheeks warmed, heat rising from deep within at this attitude of men who belittle the success of women.

"Aye, Carli, just teasing you, *lo siento*, okay?" His eyes had softened, and I could see he regretted his joke.

"Hmm hmm," I replied. "Anyway, really have to go!" I said, turning my back on both men, and heading down the sidewalk, waving goodbye by holding my hand up in the air and fluttering it, as I walked faster.

"Carli, have a great afternoon!" Said Manuel. I smiled but didn't turn around for him to see.

The gall, the insolence of Antonio! Manuel didn't think that way, did he?

Manuel had been a true ally when I opened my business, spending a week painting walls, moving furniture, building racks, and installing lighting, all things he would later not even do for his own restaurant.

Of course, that's because he had had investors and a large budget, while I scraped by, using only a fraction of my savings to open my shop. Though my parents offered to help, and I had a small trust fund, I was determined to do it on my own. And that trust fund was for retirement, not to risk on a business venture.

That thought, coupled with the recent events, inevitably led my mind to Mil and her investment in Manuel's restaurant.

Lost in thought, I didn't realize I had slowed my walk on the narrow sidewalk until other pedestrians brought me back to reality. Their impatient glances and the swiftness with which they passed me made it clear that my sluggish pace was out of place.

Embarrassed, I quickened my steps, noticing only then that I'd crossed Calle Hidalgo Macias, and was now walking alongside the wall of the Bellas Artes building. Which was past my shop.

I shook my head, trying to rid myself of the distracting thoughts, much like a dog would shake off water with a vigorous twist.

This thing would be the end of me. I needed to leave it to the professionals. The police.

No.

I had to solve the mystery so life could go back to normal, to be sure Manuel was safe. Please.

Feeling sheepish, I turned around and retraced my steps to my shop. Upon arrival, I unlocked the door and turned the sign to Open, inviting in potential customers.

I settled onto the stool behind the register, a wave of despondence washing over me.

I shook off the melancholy with a sigh, forcing myself back into business mode as the cheerful tinkle of the door's wind chime announced a customer's entrance.

When I saw who it was, my blood pressure shot up to the sky like fireworks.

CHAPTER 12

I looked around as if doing so would make other people materialize. My instinct said for me to not be alone with her.

"Janice!" I said in greeting. She hadn't said she'd be coming here; *why* was she here? At a time sure to be slow, right after comida like this. And why did she look like she'd already rehearsed something?

"Carli ... I wanted to say something to you earlier, but not outside El Café, with people around."

I gulped and waited, tipping my head to the side to urge her to go on. My fingers curled around the counter's edge.

"Of course, we have no idea what happened with Mil yet, but ... well, I hope you don't think I'd do something to her because of ... the money." She gulped, staring at me, her eyes big, body well planted as if expecting a blow.

"Why would I think that, Janice?" Keeping my face placid took a ton of energy. No little golden statuette named Oscar for me anytime soon. But growing up on the hacienda with multiple sets of parents checking the goings-on related to me and my cousins all the time, one had needed to develop a good poker face just to have a life. It still took effort for me, though.

"You were with Liam at El Café. I'm sure you two talked. I can see how you look at me now, and I know that you, and everyone else around here," at this, she swept her arm out as if to encompass the whole town and then continued, "say I took advantage of her!"

Her cheeks reddened and her voice rose higher and higher as she spoke. By the end, she wasn't screaming, but it was far from a conversational tone. Her breath came short and sharp, her words tumbling over each other like they were chasing the truth—or trying to bury it.

"*Lo siento*, Janice, so sorry, but I've never said that to anyone."

"I don't believe you! You people have no idea what I had to go through! I never meant to not pay her back. My brother lied to me! What would you do in my place?"

Her eyes had rounded to the size of 10-*peso* coins and looked shiny, like those of a glass-eyed doll.

Was Janice becoming unhinged? My eyes lowered to the counter in front of me, my mind going over her words.

"Look, Janice. The police don't even know what happened to her yet. No need to get upset like this until we have proof of something. No one is accusing you."

Poker face, poker face, poker face. The Lady Gaga song came to mind. But it couldn't drown out the thud of adrenaline in my ears.

"Yeah, well, I'm not sure I believe you, but ..." she trailed off, a balloon deflating at the end of a long party.

"It's okay, Janice. Take a deep breath. Go home and rest. Or go to the *biblioteca*; you like it there!"

The San Miguel library attracted many members of the expat community. They gathered there not only to read books, but to see shows in the small, attached theater, and to socialize in its courtyard. To catch up on gossip. Some went to teach English, others to learn Spanish.

Oops . . . as soon as I said it, I realized that it might not be the best place for Janice right now.

"Sure. The looks alone over there might kill me," she retorted, smirking.

The image was sort of funny, and when the corners of her lips lifted, mine did too, and just like that, the tension broke.

Temporarily. My muscles stayed braced.

"Would you like a coffee? Why not take a cup and enjoy it in the courtyard?" I nodded my head in its direction.

I kept a Keurig coffee maker for my regular clients, who had come to expect it while they browsed the shop.

"Nah .. I just came by to tell you that." She gazed around as she spoke, as if looking for something without knowing what. *Or*, making sure no one was watching?

Shut up! I inside screamed at the anxious voice filling my head with dark thoughts. I took a deep breath to calm myself.

"Well alright. Just say if you need something. And Janice, please don't think that way. The police will know soon what happened to her. I'm sure it was nothing. I mean, an accident of some sort, maybe she took too much of something herself without meaning to, Antonio said (had he?), or maybe something with her heart like you said."

"Antonio said that?" she asked, sounding hopeful.

Uh . . . had he?

"I think I heard him say it, *sí*? Or Manuel said he said it. Can't remember now."

Open mouth, insert foot, accuse one of my favorite people of having said something he hadn't said. Or had he? The whole affair seemed to have gathered into a big ball of confusion in my mind, a tangled tumbleweed rolling across a desert. No way to solve a crime, now was it? To crack this, I'd have to untangle things pronto!

Gather yourself, Carlota Maria Garcia Cano, like, right now.

"Oh ... okay, well, I better go." She sighed, her eyes sweeping the shop again, and I held my breath. That searching look. I didn't like it. I didn't like it one bit.

After she left, I walked over to a sofa on the other side of the store, and sank into it, not caring about the two women who had come in and were now browsing the clothes racks, talking up a storm about someone's wedding next month in New Orleans, something about the bride wearing red.

Of course, my designer mind began to create the bridesmaids' dresses in pale pink, as seen in traditional Chinese weddings when the bride wore red. But indulging in this now wouldn't get me anywhere as far as solving the mystery that had so many of us on edge.

And, Amy! I still hadn't called her! A phone call from a regular consignee had distracted me on the way to El Café.

Though I decided to call Amy right then and there, before I could get to my phone, one of the two women called out to me, so I headed their way instead.

They deliberated about whether one of them should buy a pink and camel-colored Valentino swing top and skirt suit, but the waist needed to be adjusted. They were leaving San Miguel tomorrow morning, and no way could my seamstress do it in time.

In the end, they left with the suit folded into silk paper and placed into one of my signature shopping bags. She'd have it altered at home. A good deal for buyer, seller, and of course, for my business.

I'd been about to call the consignor and ask her to lower the price once more since the suit had been here for three months already.

As I approached the counter to retrieve my phone, a man came in and asked about a gift certificate for his wife. She'd heard great things about my shop. It warmed my heart on both a personal and professional level.

Making women happy with what they wore was pure joy for me. I handed him the gift certificate in an envelope on which I'd written his wife's name in calligraphy, a skill I'd learned from my American grandmother, and used for this and for birthday cards.

Finally by myself, I picked up the phone and dialed Amy. Voicemail picked up, to my disappointment, and I left a message. Her greeting said she was in Dallas with her husband and would return on Friday. She had not told me they were going, but they often went on the spur of the moment. I'd have to wait to know about the seating chart, unless I called her U.S. number, which I had. Somewhere ...

But just then, three women came through the door, doing their best to out-talk one another. The shop was getting busier and busier, and it might be time to see about having Esme full-time in the afternoons or hiring someone else for the days she didn't work. I took a deep breath and greeted them.

A few minutes later, as they browsed and chatted, I stood at the register going through sales receipts for the past two days to see who I needed to pay for their consigned merchandise.

Suddenly, something one of the women said stopped me cold.

They spoke in stage-whispers, but I heard every word.

"The woman I spoke to said she'd been murdered, poisoned, is what she said. No one liked her, apparently." Said one of them.

What? I asked myself. What?

How had these tourists learned of a death in our inner circle? Surely, no Música Clásica Esencial member would gossip about such a thing with tourists! All the locals, especially those who earned a living here, realized how detrimental this could be to all of us. And no one knew yet what Mil had died of. Speculate, speculate—all anyone did.

The rumor mill in this town made me *loca*. Sometimes, the cattiness of the New York fashion world had nothing on it.

Some liked the controversy or loved pretending to know things they knew nothing about. As if it gave them some sort of status. In my opinion, the only status it gave them was that of being known as magpies—the kind who spread false information.

But wait? Isn't this what I'd told myself Janice might do? If she were spreading this rumor already, then surely, she hadn't done it? Or maybe she wanted the rumor out there to deflect attention.

I found a reason to get closer to them and to hear what else they would say. Were they really talking about Mil?

"Wow,' said a second voice, "imagine being at a party and someone offs you."

No kidding. But who would have told this woman such a thing? Mil hadn't died at the party. Just, perhaps, as a result of something she'd had to drink while there.

If curiosity could kill humans too, I'd surely die right now. The thought heated my face; this was no time to ponder death.

"Well, my sister said she thought some people might want her, you know, out of the way. People who owed her money, things like that."

Her sister? Who might her sister be? I peeked a bit to see if she bore a resemblance to anyone I knew, but no one came to mind.

"Oh look," she added, reverence in her voice, "a Versace body suit! My daughter would look great in this. What size is it?" She continued, though clearly talking to herself. She looked at the tag, then continued her monologue.

"Perfect, it's her size!" She said out loud, then reverted to stage-whispering. "Wow, I can't believe I can get it for this price!"

She looked around, spotted me by the register, and called me over. I guess I'd now never find out who her sister was, or what else she'd said about Mil.

In the end, the woman opted to not buy the body suit because there was a teeny-tiny barely there lighter spot, smaller than a one-peso coin, below the waistline, where no one would see it; it's why we'd discounted it so low.

But who was spreading this rumor? Okay, I'd been thinking those things too, but in private. Not blabbing them about town.

This called for serious sleuthing.

Janice spent every Saturday night she wasn't attending a music event with the same three friends, all single women. They would indulge in a nice dinner at an upscale Centro restaurant, then go to one of the many small bars with live music. She'd often brag about staying out 'til the wee hours, despite being sixty-five years old. No concert was scheduled for tonight.

What if I went to her house, and ... well, see what I could see? She didn't have pets, and I had a key because I'd once sent my maid to water her plants when she'd been out of town. Janice had asked me to keep the key in case she ever needed to go away and couldn't find a house sitter, as sometimes happened.

No doubt I blushed to a deep crimson, thinking about entering the woman's house without her permission. But how else was I going to get answers? To find out who'd done it, if anyone had, I needed to eliminate my suspects one at a time until one of them became impossible to eliminate due to too much evidence.

Yes, okay, I'd start with her. I liked Janice well enough, but my bond to Manuel was love and family. So he had to come first.

Speaking of Manuel, I called him to claim fatigue, and asked that he not come over. We'd rescheduled our glass of wine meeting to tonight, but this was more important to ensure future glasses-of-wine-on-my-couch evenings with him. I mean, how could I say, Manuel, I wonder if you killed Mil, or, I'm looking for the real killer to reassure myself you didn't do it.

Of course, I trusted him. Of course, he had not killed her. But the police might need convincing if no evidence pointed to others should it come back that Mil died from something in the wine.

The ex-cop in Manuel wouldn't want me breaking into any-one's house for any reason, even if it was to save him. He was such an upright man. I puzzled this out in my head for a while. He was upright. So why was I investigating Mil's murder to reassure myself he wasn't the one who killed her?

Because. Hadn't someone said that we never really knew anyone all that well?

I'd wait until nine o'clock when Janice would be out for sure. It wouldn't do to run into her on her short street in her neighborhood of the Colonia San Antonio. My only reason for being there could only be to go to her house.

After mulling it over, I decided to take a taxi since the sun sank below the horizon around seven-thirty at this time of year. The chances of Janice finding out I'd taken a taxi to her street tonight were as good as her finding out what kind of chili peppers Manuel used in his famous chicken mole. None at all.

The cab dropped me off in front of her house, and for good measure, I pressed the doorbell. If she was at home, I'd say I'd stopped by to ask how she was doing, considering how upset she'd been earlier.

Her key weighed in my hand, a bold reminder of the risk I was taking. I rang the bell once more, and my heartbeat quickened.

Could I really do this? Enter her house without permission? My hands trembled. My conscience nagged at me.

No one came to the door.

My breath shaky, I let myself into her courtyard, my heart pounding fast and loud—a frantic rhythm I feared could be heard all the way into Centro. A light sweat gathered on my brow. I urged my heart to slow down, but it wouldn't listen.

I followed the path, bordered by meticulously pruned shrubs, while pink bougainvillea trailed down the wall on the right, their honeysuckle-like scent filling the air, their delicate petals almost glowing in the soft light. They whispered warnings to me as I passed by ...

Finally, I reached her front door. Again, I paused, listening for any sign of life inside. Knocked on the door. Only silence answered. I took a deep breath, smelling and tasting the crisp outside air, inserted the key into the lock and turned the doorknob, the brass cool under my fingers.

With a soft creak of the door, I stepped into the unknown. My senses heightened, every sound and smell magnified. The house seemed to hold its breath, waiting to see what I would do next.

CHAPTER 13

O nce inside, my heart beating like a jackhammer, I nearly turned around to leave. What was I thinking, coming into her home without permission? Would karma get me for this? No, that was Amy's belief, not mine; no such thing existed, but what if ...?

I stood in the foyer, taking a few breaths. The smell of whatever Janice had cooked earlier, something with garlic, which always lingered long in the air, wafted over to me from down the hallway despite the kitchen being at the back of the large colonial house.

Her home spoke of traditional Mexican houses with Saltillo tile on the floors, and *boveda* ceilings in several rooms. Add the modernized kitchen with its stainless-steel appliances, granite countertops, and American contemporary furniture, and it gave the house a nice eclectic vibe.

Not sure where to start, I wandered into the living room, sinking for a moment into the embrace of a bright orange couch. It faced a windowed wall with a door leading to a private courtyard. After some thought, I headed to the master bedroom on this floor to explore.

I saw quickly that she hadn't moved back into it since her brother's passing, the air stagnant, the room untouched.

She had let him use her bedroom so he could avoid the stairs once he got weaker. Maybe memories of his stay made it hard for her to reclaim the space, especially since he'd betrayed her.

Personally, if someone close to me had died in my bedroom, I'd need time and a thorough renovation before using the room again. My body shuddered, a chill running down my spine.

There was nothing in any of the dresser drawers, little in the closets. It looked like Janice had already given away, or discarded, her brother's possessions.

Standing in the room, I hoped for clarity but felt uneasy in the deceased man's bedroom. The silence weighed on me. What if his spirit appeared? Shaking off the thought, I moved to the connected bathroom. It was nearly empty, with no sign of prescription pills. But who's to say Janice had used prescription pills to poison Mil? If she'd poisoned Mil ...

I then searched the kitchen, specifically the spice cabinet, the smell of spices nearly overwhelming when I opened its door. It'd be a clever spot to hide poison, *sí*? As long as one didn't accidentally flavor a dish with it, that is.

I examined various bottles, ensuring the contents matched their labels. Not a fake one in the bunch, as far as I could see. Or smell, that is.

Let's see, where else? Ah, upstairs, of course. I climbed the staircase, a hand resting on the cool, polished banister, nerves on edge. The silent climb, due to stone steps, heightening my anticipation nonetheless, and I felt sillier and sillier as I went.

What was I doing here, invading Janice's space?

I entered the bathroom first, where the mild scent of a citrus cleaner teased at my nostrils. The cabinets, two of them, had only one prescription bottle, an anti-depressant, though I didn't recognize its name, probably a generic version of Zoloft, the label smooth under my fingers.

So, Janice took an anti-depressant? This was not my business, and guilt gripped me, a sensation much like a cold hand touching my heart, for now knowing this very personal infor-mation about her.

In the first bedroom, there was a small desk in the corner with four drawers, two on each side. The faint creak of the wooden floor followed me as I approached and checked the left drawer. Empty.

When I opened the bottom right drawer, I found a large manila envelope, typically used for mailing unfolded legal documents, serving as the drawer's liner. It lay beneath mis-cellaneous office supplies, the shuffle of a notepad and gentle clatter of pens and paper clips breaking the silence. I felt the texture of these things with my fingertips, so common and ordinary, yet now charged with meaning.

I contemplated how to retrieve the envelope without moving the items resting on it, but it was clear I couldn't access it without shifting them.

Careful y, I moved the office supplies, each sound they made echoing in the quiet room and unnerving me.

With shaking hands, I opened the slender envelope, revealing a single sheet of paper. My fingers trembled against its crisp edges, and my heart thudded rapidly as I scanned through it, my eyes not believing what I read.

And that's when the sound of someone talking downstairs reached me. Janice!

CHAPTER 14

M y heart slammed against my rib cage loudly, reverberating in my ears. I couldn't make out what she said, only that she was speaking.

Why was she home already? Was she coming upstairs?

I looked around for a place to hide, overwhelmed with a sense of panic, but saw nowhere that would work.

The room closed in on me, each piece of furniture seeming to laugh, mocking me for being there.

This was *her* bedroom. She'd find me. Fast. No matter where I hid. Would she call the police? I felt my face turn the red of a stoplight at the thought of Antonio learning my "adventure."

My breathing came in ragged gasps, scenting the surrounding air with the fear that consumed me.

Adrenaline rushed through me, propelled through my whole being as if by a tsunami wave.

Instinct took over. I tiptoed from the bedroom, pausing at the top of the stairs, each step I took a careful dance fueled by anxiety, by desperation, the floor cool beneath my feet, every sound around me menacing.

From the distant murmur of her voice, I could tell Janice had moved to the back of the house.

Despite the distance, I heard the gurgling sound of water being poured from a five-gallon water jug, present in most homes in Mexico, soon followed by the distinct click-click-click of a gas stove burner.

Oddly, in that tense moment, I found myself noting the house's peculiar acoustics that seemed to amplify sounds, grateful for it because it turned ordinary noises into clues about her movements.

She kept on talking, pausing now and then. I could now tell that she was alone and talking on the phone. Perhaps the conversation would distract her enough for me to make my escape.

Holding my breath, ears straining to catch every nuance of sound, shoes in hand, I began my descent down the cool, stone staircase—thankful for their silence, with no betraying creaks.

But when I had both feet on the second step and was about to step on the third, Janice's voice got louder and her silhouette emerged in the hallway, forcing me to retreat to the landing and put my back against its far wall, my hands flat against it, its rough texture pressing into my palms.

My heart pounded in my chest, terrified that she'd ascend the stairs. My breathing shallow, I slipped into the second bedroom, which I hoped she didn't enter often. The scent of disuse and dust met me, and I felt better about using it as a hiding place. I left the door slightly ajar and listened.

I breathed a quiet sigh of relief when, due to the change in the sound of her voice, I realized that she'd gone into the living room, my heart still dancing way too fast, its rhythm an insistent drumbeat. I tried to will it to calm so I could think, so I could breathe easier, my throat now dry and tense.

Soon after, I heard a squeak I could tell came from the courtyard patio door opening, thanks once again to the house's peculiar acoustics. Her voice faded, telling me she'd stepped outside.

I seized my opportunity and darted back downstairs, the air parting around me as I rushed, my feet barely touching the steps.

The front door beckoned just to the left at the base of the staircase, a vantage point hidden from her view, even if she were to return into the living room. With one last glance over my shoulder, I made my escape.

I gently shut the door behind me, fearful that my racing heart and trembling limbs would give me away. The latch clicked into place, quietly.

Staying low, the cooler night air hitting me, I only rose to sprint toward the street door after rounding the first bend in the courtyard's path, the paving stones keeping my escape silent.

I quickly let myself out onto the street. Despite my shaky hands and reddened face, I tried to maintain a façade of normalcy.

The weight of what I'd done settled like boulders in my stomach in complete opposition to the familiar sights and sounds of the street.

A man strolled along the opposite sidewalk, his footsteps a soft patter on the cobblestones. He glanced at the shoes in my hands, his eyes widening, then moving quickly to my face, then away just as fast, clearly of a mind to not meddle. He looked like a normal middle-class person, not a bandito, and kept on walking, his shoulders slightly tense, perhaps because my appearance had startled him.

That's when I realized I'd not thought of how I'd get home after my little unauthorized visit.

I put my shoes back on, grateful for the support as they encased my feet, and headed in the same direction as the man, following about fifty feet behind.

He seemed headed for Centro based on him turning left when he got to the end of the street. Was he a neighbor? Would he ask Janice about the woman who'd left her house with shoes in hand tonight?

A knot of worry formed in my gut. I quickened my pace, eager for the brighter lights and activity of Ancha de San Antonio, just a few blocks away.

What a foolhardy move on my part. If I couldn't plan my investigating any better than this, then how could I save Manuel?

But, wait. I had planned well. Janice never came home early on Saturday nights. She said so herself all the time.

So, why tonight? When I'd chosen to snoop around her house? This thought caused a hot flush to spread across my cheeks. But if it hadn't been for her unexpected return, I'd have had my shoes on when I exited the property, and wouldn't have caught that questioning glance from the passerby.

Once I reached the main artery, I hailed a taxi to avoid waiting for Uber, the familiar streets a comfort to me. The man who had seen me leaving Janice's had veered off into a side street. The thought of him nagged at me, weighing at the back of my mind. Did he know her?

Once inside my own front door, the tension left my body and I let out a big sigh of relief, double checking that I'd locked, and dead bolted the door. I poured myself a serving of red wine and sank deep into the couch, the plush cushions wrapping around me. Dap almost immediately jumped onto my lap, his fur soft and comforting against my body. Soon, his purring filled the room like a small engine, a soothing background melody that brought me back to a calmer state of mind.

So. What could I do about the letter I'd seen at Janice's?

I pondered my next move. For about five seconds. Then, realization hit me like lightning. I shot up from the couch and felt the right pocket of the skinny jeans I'd worn for my playing detective, the hairs on the back of my next standing on end. Dap meowed furiously at being so disturbed, jumped off the couch too, and sauntered away, giving me a cat's equivalent of a dirty look over his shoulder.

I had not just read the letter ... in my sudden panic when Janice returned, I'd instinctively shoved it into my pocket before returning the envelope and the office supplies to the drawer.

And now, feeling into my pocket, the faint crinkle of a wad of paper under my fingertips confirmed it.

I had the letter!

CHAPTER 15

The following day, with the weight of melancholy lingering over me from the ordeal at Janice's, and the evidence in that letter churning in my mind like in a restless sea, I yearned for my childhood home. The hacienda where the scent of blooming flowers filled the air, where I rode horses, played with cousins, and where, as a teen, I learned of *mamá*'s profound grief over my bio-father, each memory bittersweet and warm at the same time.

When people looked at my family, they probably saw an idyllic situation. But every family has its heartaches, its challenges, its embarrassments. Including mine.

Would this possible new situation with Manuel cause another one?

Ah, the scandals. For instance, whenever my mother mentioned my bio-father, her voice softened and cracked, as if breaking under the weight of lost love. This, despite the love she felt for my *papá*.

My mother and bio father had met when he'd come to San Miguel for work, had fallen deeply in love, and become engaged with the blessing of my *abuelos*.

Eager to merge their worlds, he'd gone to Austin to seek his own parents' blessing. While they joyously prepared to visit San Miguel and meet my mother and *abuelos*, fate had intervened the day before the trip. A reckless semi-truck driver snatched my father's life, while he, the truck driver, emerged alive.

Two months passed before my heartbroken *mamá* discovered a new life growing in her belly. Me. A scandal of major proportions back then, a secret whispered through the family, rustling through our gossip grapevine like a chilly wind.

To avoid another family disgrace, upon discovering her pregnancy, my *abuelos* had insisted on a marriage between my mother and Alfonso.

Out of respect for the man I considered my father and who had given me only love and treated me as if I were his biological daughter, he would never know that I spoke to my bio-father.

In an old photo I had of him with my mother, their eyes shimmered with unmistakable love, overshadowing everything else, like sunlight piercing through a stormy sky.

Wher troubled, I'd talk to him, holding that image close, its edges worn soft from holding it countless times, the sensation a comfort, seeking his guidance.

I now reached into my night table where I kept the photo hidden, and holding it close to my heart, I returned to the living room, flopped into the couch, Dap curled next to me, matcha tea at the ready, its earthy sweet aroma mingling with my emotions.

Holding the photo with both hands, and looking into his clear, piercing blue eyes, eyes I saw every morning in the mirror, their depth pulling me in, I asked, my lips moving in a near-silent whisper.

Dad, did Manuel do this? Did he kill a woman to save himself from having to pay back his debt to her?

I closed my eyes, eyes glistening as they often did when I held this photo, and took a moment to collect myself. And then, I waited, my body still, my whole being straining for a sign, a feeling. And wincing at the audacity of my question, at the disloyalty to Manuel.

But nothing came at all, the silence almost a physical presence, heavy and cold. I sometimes felt guidance from him. Only not this time ...

With no answers as to how to resolve this, confused about the whole thing, my thoughts a knotted string in my mind, I decided to go to the hacienda for Sunday comida, knowing that family and tradition would act as a balm to my troubled soul.

And who knew? Perhaps some information had found its way into the rumor mill of my family. Yes, I realized being obsessed over solving a murder that might not even have happened bordered on the ridiculous, but the urgency of the situation gnawed at my heart, and one must be prepared when one wanted—needed—to save a loved one.

Of course, if I'd only known what information I was about to find out, I might not have gone to my ancestral home. Because it only complicated things, solidified my fears about Manuel.

I pulled into the familiar circular drive, gravel crunching beneath the tires, the sunlight casting playful shadows on it. Before me, bathed in the gentle early afternoon light, stood the comforting silhouette of my childhood home. The light hum of the car's engine subsided as I turned it off, and the chirping of daytime birds took its place, a soothing welcome.

As I opened the car door, a warm breeze carried the rich and familiar scent of roses towards me—roses my father had planted along one side of the driveway to surprise my mother on their first wedding anniversary, their fragrance a tangible connection to love and family.

The serene symphony of a Sunday at the hacienda enveloped me: in addition to the birds, leaves gently rustled in nearby trees, children's laughter floated toward me from somewhere on the property, and I heard the faint buzzing of bees.

Every time I returned, no matter how brief my absence, it revived in me a deep appreciation for our home's enduring beauty. It was one of two main houses on the property, built by my great-great-grandfather. His brother, Manuel's great-great-grandfather, had built the other main house.

Because they were on equal footing in their ownership of the property, the brothers had wanted houses of equal stature for their families.

Though smaller and simpler than typical hacienda homes, the impeccable craftsmanship and materials of our homes, bathed in warm hues, were irreplaceable testaments to history and love.

At this hour, the early afternoon sun kissed the house's facade, granting it an ethereal halo that always tugged at my heartstrings.

As if on cue, the door opened, revealing my parents' radiant smiles, beaming just for me from the verandah.

These two always made me feel like the most important person in their world.

"Mamá!" I exclaimed, taking in her elegance in the sky-blue silk Ralph Lauren dress I'd chosen for her. It ended just at her knees, complementing her salt and pepper hair elegantly tied in a bun. The only jewelry she wore was the eye-catching diamond ring from Papá. She rarely wore it at home, usually only when they entertained.

I held on to her like onto a life raft when we hugged.

Papá, not wanting to miss out, joined us in a heartfelt group embrace, filling the moment with laughter. One would think we hadn't seen each other in months, instead of just ten days.

"*Hola, mi hija bonita,*" they both said, speaking over one another. Though them greeting me as their "beautiful daughter" sounded corny to me, I found it endearing, anyway.

We went inside and sat in the spacious living room, except for Mamá, who continued to the kitchen to help Maria, our "long-suffering maid," as I sometimes teased her, and at which she always tsk-tsked with a smile. To me, Maria was as much a part of the hacienda as my parents, the beauty of the land, and synonymous with the wonderful smells that always greeted me as I entered the kitchen, her kitchen, one where, as a young child, I'd followed her around, pestering her for sweets or other treats. She had not always given in to me, but had always been kind when she'd said "no."

Maria and Mamá soon arrived, Maria holding a tray filled with French coffee presses, and Mamá carrying another laden with pastries—enough to feed an army. When I saw Maria, memories from my childhood rushed back. I stood and embraced her, recalling all the times she'd comforted me with such hugs whenever I'd come to her with scrapes and bruises.

My parents and I spoke of Mil, the big news in town. The conversation then meandered over to Manuel, the restaurant, and what would happen to Mil's investment in it.

"One of those notes on the restaurant is due in about a month, if I remember it right."

My ears perked up.

"You mean ... you mean the money Millicent lent to Manuel?"

Papá nodded as he took a sip of coffee.

"Alejandro said that it can be renegotiated if she were to die."

"Oh, but is that good or bad, do you think?"

He shrugged.

"Depends on what Manuel wants, and the heirs. Though I assume it's just her son, right?"

He looked at me as if I'd have the answer.

"I'm not sure. I would think so from what I know of her."

What if Manuel didn't have the money? It felt as if a herd of horses were running inside my head.

It made no sense that this man, whom I'd known all my life, would do this. But then, life often made no sense. We all did crazy things when life pushed us into corners we couldn't fight our way out of. As I'd learned in New York.

"Papá, does Manuel not have the ..."

Suddenly, the sound of boots echoed in the air when José, the foreman, rushed onto the verandah and into the living room, urgently seeking my father about a doe in labor.

Oh, yay, I thought, more goat cheese, but I stamped down the not-so-nice thought, recalling all the people on the land who made a living from it.

"Joining us?" Papá asked, a mischievous glint in his eye.

I declined with a smile, still haunted by a childhood memory. At age six, I'd watched a difficult goat birth from behind hay bales, where a breech baby was swung vigorously to clear its lungs. I'd mistakenly seen it as cruelty. Even after bonding with the newborn over the first few weeks of its life, I couldn't bring myself to witness another birth.

Within an hour, all the friends and relatives arrived bearing food. children, babies, and good cheer.

Now and then, a waft of enticing aromas danced through the air—the rich, smoky scent of meats grilling, intermingling with the earthy and piquant fragrances from the various side dishes.

It was a culinary tapestry, each dish representing a family member's contribution: pozole, spicy salsas, creamy guacamoles, steamed tamales, frijoles charros, fresh salads, and *aguas frescas*. The shared feast seemed to epitomize the spirit of unity and community.

Children ran around on the lawn, their laughter a delightful melody. Every so often, a ball would roll onto the verandah, only to be swiftly retrieved by giggling culprits.

I spoke to Amelia, who had been invited by a cousin who attended school with her. She was the daughter of expats I knew vaguely, and she'd been at the Música Clásica Esencial party with her parents. And they'd been sitting at the table next to Mil's with Lisa Martin, Denise Bouchard, and their husbands.

Yes, the table with that notorious glass of red wine.

She relayed something Denise had said, as they'd been at the same table. It felt like it meant something, but I couldn't pinpoint what.

I wanted to talk to her some more, but just then a three-year-old cousin, all wobbly legs and a head full of black curls, presented me with two wilted flowers, her big brown mischievous eyes taking up much of her face, shouting, "Tatie!" her name for me, unable to say Carli.

My heart melted and thoughts of murders, blame, and the problem of what to do about Manuel swooshed right out of my head, like a girl dancing her way out of the room at her *quinceañera* to avoid a boy of whom she's not fond, but with whom her father wants her to dance.

I picked up little Abril and hugged her to me, but she wriggled free, giggling. I put her down, and she grabbed my hand to drag me—though she didn't have to work too hard at it—toward the large children's playground at the side of the house. Her aim turned out to be the swings, so I placed her in one and pushed a few times until her mother came looking for her. I handed pushing duties to her, and returned to the verandah to say my goodbyes, which would take the better part of an hour.

The whole day and into the early evening when I left, spent, but also energized from catching up with aunts, uncles, cousins, nieces, nephews—and thinking I wouldn't need to eat for a week—thoughts of Manuel and the money coming due swam around in my head. He'd not been at comida, having had to be at the restaurant to prepare for a party of twenty celebrating a birthday this evening, so I couldn't ask him. And, anyway, why ask a question to which you feared the answer?

On the ride home, I tried to clear my mind of everything other than warm thoughts of my family and enjoy the beautiful countryside.

My phone buzzed from the passenger seat, and I glanced at the display. Oh ... wasn't Manuel hyper-busy with that dinner party?

"Manuel, *que tal*?" I asked when I picked up.

"Hey, *linda* Carlita!"

"Don't you have a dinner to put together, *vato*?" I often referred to him, and my other male cousins, as "dude" in Spanish.

"*Sí*, taking a break. Wondering about the family rumor mill. What's new with everybody?"

Now, I knew Manuel well enough that no way was he calling to get the latest installment of the Cano Telenovela. No, he wanted to know if anyone had mentioned anything about the wine.

"Manuel, no one knows besides you and me ..." I began, but he interrupted me.

"You never know. I worry someone else saw. I mean ... well ... never mind."

Never mind what? What had he been about to say? My foot relaxed off the accelerator so that my car decelerated, and a driver following me too close honked. Well, he should keep his distance! We were entering Centro—I'd just made a sharp left onto Calle de la Garza—no place to drive fifty miles per hour!

"I see," was all I could think of saying while I raised all my windows, slowed down, and hugged the right curb so the angry driver could pass me, which he did promptly, honking again.

"Everything okay?" Asked Manuel.

"Yes, just a crazy driver. He's gone now."

"Have you heard from Antonio?" I asked him, to say something, anything, except to ask the one question to which I wanted an answer.

Someone in the background on Manuel's end called out to him, and he covered the mouthpiece while he answered.

"I have to go, Prima," was all he said when he uncovered his phone. He was already talking to the other person as he hung up.

I drove to my usual parking spot and left the car. The noise of the town swelled around me, as I strolled the few blocks home, car exhaust fumes filling the air, while disturbing thoughts filled my head.

Even if Manuel hadn't done it, someone had. I now felt certain her death could not have been natural, a cold realization settling in my stomach.

The murder of an upstanding member of the expat community could spell trouble for the shops and restaurants who relied not only on tourism, but on wealthier locals, including expats.

The city had been built on a bedrock of rose quartz, a stone celebrated not just for its ability to dispel negative energy on a spiritual plane, but also as a symbol of love, peace, and serenity.

San Miguel attracted a diverse group of expatriates, including healers, artists, writers, painters, potters, and other creative, mild-mannered individuals. They valued peace and serenity, and definitely safety, which seemed to all be in short supply lately.

Increasing incidents of violence, especially against their own, would unsettle them, and possibly compel them to leave, or discourage others from coming, threatening the town's economic fabric.

It would be a monumental scandal, putting everyone on edge, like watching a storm brewing on the horizon—uncertain how things would stand once it hit and passed.

A storm the size of which Amelia, a political science student, or any diplomat, would be hard put to fix with pretty words ...

CHAPTER 16

I woke up the next morning to the rhythmic sound of rain tapping on my bedroom window, feeling languorous. For a moment, I let myself melt into it. It was the kind of morning that made you want to disappear under the covers with a sketch pad or a book—but there was no time for that.

Dapper rose from the foot of the bed, and strutted over to me, his paws making soft indentations on the plush duvet. He hopped onto my chest to stare into my eyes.

"Dap, ouch ..." I said, surprised. The slight pressure of his paws felt intentional. He rarely behaved this way—on the couch, yes, but not here in bed. It seemed as if he wanted to tell me something.

"Are you hungry, *mi corazón?*"

Meow was the only response—of course—the sound echoing softly, almost like a question. I made to get up, but he resisted, so I stayed, looking into his eyes, as gray as a deep ocean. I petted his luxurious black coat, cool silk under my fingers, half-heartedly, still sleepy. The moment stretched. My mind wandered.

His head swiveled toward the window, distracted by noise that seemed to come from the garden of the house behind mine, and I turned my head to look at my bedside alarm clock; six.

Plenty of time for my usual morning matcha ritual.

I grabbed my silk robe (Dior, vintage) from the settee at the foot of my bed, wrapping myself in its glorious cashmere warmth, allowing myself a moment to sink into its embrace.

And then it hit. Mil. Manuel. Janice. The letter. The money coming due. My heart jolted, as if hit by an electric shock.

I meandered toward the bathroom, where my eyes drifted to the deep-soaking tub. There was time for a short bath, maybe, which in my world meant thirty minutes.

I then strolled to the kitchen where my morning matcha tea ritual called to me. I walked slower than usual, caught between the comfort of routine and the weight of what lay ahead.

I filled the electric kettle and turned it on to heat the water to one-hundred-sixty degrees, the ideal temperature for the perfect cup of green tea.

While I waited, I gazed out the kitchen window, which, being on the second floor, gave me a clear view of the garden of the home just behind mine, which belonged to the Gonzalez family. Of course, this brought back Amy and Douglas's garden, the party, and the incident that had become a gnawing itch in the back of my mind.

Pink bougainvillea burst and flourished along the communal wall I shared with my neighbor. Gardeners came twice per week to keep their large backyard looking like a miniature version of El Charco del Ingenio, the well-known botanical garden on the outskirts of town.

I never tired of this morning view while waiting for the water to heat, the colors meshing in a natural palette, a reminder of Mother Earth's simple gifts.

My phone buzzed, vibrating softly, creating a micro-earthquake on the counter. Antonio. Seeing his name on the display, I let it go. If I took his call right now, it might derail my whole day. Or confirm my worst fears.

I gazed at my phone, wondering if he now knew about Manuel giving Mil that glass of wine. I sighed deeply, the air rushing from my lungs like from a deflating balloon. It was done. The only thing now was to ensure Manuel's freedom. No matter what might have happened . . . what he might have done.

The thought weighed me down, exhausting me. The kettle beeped, its high-pitched chime bringing me back to my task.

I preheated my flowered ceramic mug with hot water and prepped the beaker with matcha, mushroom powders, ashwagandha, astragalus, coconut oil, and raw honey from the hives at the *hacienda*.

No one else made it quite like I did. After blending, there it was. Voilà! My signature latte. Manuel and others disliked it, but its earthy taste, to me, was unbeatable.

Dap meowed, a clarion call for attention. Even though I'd fed him, he got two chicken treats. I mean, he had so few pleasures in life. We then continued our morning routine to the rooftop terrace.

I settled into my favorite chair on the roof deck, tea by my side and, closing my eyes, took two deep breaths of the cooler outside air, then reopened them, looking straight ahead this time.

And enjoyed the iconic view of the Parroquia de San Miguel Arcángel, all of San Miguel clustered around it like a clutch of chicks tight around its mother hen. People from all over the world came to see the beautiful pink church, and with good reason.

While Dap basked in a sunbeam, I savored my first sip of tea, its earthy scent both warming and calming. Nearby roof dogs barked, punctuating the otherwise quiet morning. The dogs, common in San Miguel, acted as security against thieves. And drove our expat neighbors crazy.

Eventually, I poured a quick bath and dropped in the usual blend of lemon and peppermint oils—part comfort, part alarm clock. I slid under the water up to my chin and closed my eyes.

Immediately, all the players in the mystery of Mil's death began to parade in my head. I placed my focus on each of the three in turn.

Janice ... what I'd found incriminated her, but it still wasn't proof enough that she'd done it. The courts would call the letter strong circumstantial evidence, but most likely couldn't convict on just that. Could they? What else might I have found if she hadn't interrupted me?

The essential oils did their job, and I became more alert.

If Janice had done it, wouldn't she have appeared more nervous when she'd come to the shop? She simply seemed as if she wanted to be sure no one saw her as a murderess.

And whatever conversation she'd been having when she'd arrived before I finished my search, and though I couldn't hear the exact words, her voice had remained upbeat.

I moved my hands through the water, and the ripples it created mirrored my disjointed thoughts.

Still, that letter had to mean something ...

I couldn't share this information with Antonio. Because how would I explain how I got it? Same with Manuel.

Nevertheless, it moved Janice to the top of my suspect list.

The water cooled. Reality calling me back.

Ah, why was Luna not here right now? I needed her! She'd know what to do. I wished she were here and not in Mexico City working on that project. And this was something that could only be discussed in person.

My phone rang and vibrated, the buzz echoing against the tiled walls, but I'd left it on the vanity and couldn't see who was calling. Whoever it was would have to wait.

And what about Liam? I'd found nothing on him, but maybe I hadn't tried hard enough? Wasn't it true that oftentimes, the murderer was close to the victim? That's what Antonio and Manuel said all the time. But then, Janice had been close to her at one time. And Manuel ...

What if I snuck into Mil's house and poked around a bit like I'd done at Janice's?

My heart thundered like a jet taking off, but really, how else would I get any information other than by snooping?

Getting into her house, now Liam's, wasn't really possible, though. I didn't have a key, for one. Besides, the thought unsettled me, a dissonant element in an otherwise perfect rendition of a piece of music. Add to that the possibility of having an "adventure" like I'd had at Janice's ...

If the autopsy revealed someone had poisoned or otherwise killed Millicent, the police would go to Liam first. In another epiphany, I realized Antonio had said nothing about the condition in which they had found Mil.

Would he have told Manuel or me if she'd been, say, strangled, or shot, or stabbed? Or looked like a person who had been poisoned? Well, he had said as much to Manuel. But what *did* that look like? I wondered.

The cop in him prohibited his telling us too much, and the cousin in him, tempted as he might be, couldn't say anything either because he was a cop. Even though he and Manuel had once been colleagues, they no longer were. And the body had been sent to Querétaro ...

I wondered what Liam did all day while waiting for the autopsy results. He wouldn't get a death certificate until then. Which meant nothing could be done about her estate yet.

There were no doctors' appointments to ferry his mother to, no *comidas* or dinners in restaurants to escort her to. Her friends and acquaintances were certainly calling the house to give their condolences, but other than that, what might take him away from home for an extended period? How might I find out?

Did I dare go when he was out? With relief, I realized that even if I mustered the courage, I couldn't easily break into his house. No key.

Next ... Manuel. My innards twisted each time I recalled he might have deliberately done this. No amount of untangling could loosen this knot. Thinking of him in that light crushed me. What if he was proven guilty? My heart sank, a rock falling to the bottom of an ocean.

Why hadn't he said anything to me about the loan? We told one another everything. Or so I'd believed. Hmm ... well, I wasn't telling him my suspicions about his involvement in all this.

If only I could find out whether he had the money without asking him. Who might tell me that? My father. The whole of my body resisted this. I mean, once I knew, I knew.

What if it turned out he had to ask his father for the money? His pride would never allow it. Might he choose to commit murder instead? Tension rose in my chest, an invisible hand squeezing my heart.

He had opened his restaurant business against his parents' wishes, after all. Though they had relented and now supported him in his dream, it didn't mean Manuel would consider asking them for help, especially not of the money kind.

Besides asking Mil for an extension—something else his stupid pride wouldn't allow—what were his options?

The question hung in the air like a pending storm cloud. One I hoped would never unleash upon us all.

With regret, I got out of the tub, the water now much too cool to enjoy. And I did have a business to run, after all.

And a murder to solve.

Yet, I'd made no progress on that front. I would call Antonio back, all innocent, and ask for an update.

Because that second call was him. Again.

CHAPTER 17

I got Antonio on the phone.

"Hola Antonio, *qué pasa?"* I greeted him when he answered, holding my breath. Anxiety churned in my stomach, a storm building up.

"Carli! *Hola!"*

Well, he sounded upbeat, so his calls hadn't been about what I'd expected. My tension began to dissolve, the way sugar would in a hot beverage.

"Why you are calling me at this time on a Monday, *vato?"* I asked, playing along with his good mood, fake-angry, but really, still hiding my fear that he would ask about the wine.

He laughed, the sound a soothing balm over a burn. My jaw unclenched.

"I want you to squeeze a dinner into your busy schedule."

"Oh ... what's going on?" I asked, now curious.

"Well ..." he suddenly sounded shy. "It's time I introduce my new lady to a couple of us, you know, ease her into *nuestro loco circo de familia*." Our crazy family circus. "Slowly," he added.

I imagined him shrugging after he said it.

That made me smile. Bringing someone new into our vast family was a phased approach. Step One was usually a dinner out with just a few cousins. Then came what we called The First Comida, or Step Two. If that went well, it led to Step Three, dinner with the parents.

Before this happened, parents had formed an opinion and gauged that of other family members, much like a chef carefully watching as others tasted a new dish for the first time. Any hesitation, and the formal dinner would never occur.

"But why tell me so early in the morning?" I asked.

"Oh, she's going to Mexico City Wednesday morning for business. She'll be gone a week, and I promised her we'd do this before she goes, but ... okay, I forgot because I've been busy with the Millicent Jones case. It's tomorrow night."

I ignored his reason for not remembering because I didn't want to talk about the case other than to know about the results of the autopsy. He'd tell me if those were ready. *Sí?*

"Well, well," I said, scanning my phone calendar. "I can do it, sure. Who else is coming?"

"Manuel, of course. And that's it."

"He can come? Oh, right, he's closed tomorrow. Why no one else?"

"Ah, told her I'd keep it very small."

"Alright, works for me."

"Bueno. Seven o'clock! I text you where once I know. My lady is still deciding where she wants me to take her," he chuckled.

His voice rang with excitement and pride, and it made me smile again. Antonio might be in love! The sound of his joy lessened a lot of the misgivings I'd been having about him. But not enough to confide what I knew that he might not yet know. Not yet at least.

"Okay, *vato*, see you later." I hung up the phone and let relief wash over me. It felt as if a cool breeze had blown in and lessened the heat of a hot day.

Then I remembered that soon, Antonio might have to arrest Manuel, or at least question him, depending on what the coroner said. And the smile slipped off my face. It wouldn't happen. Would it?

My phone vibrated with a text, and I startled when I saw Antonio's name.

> Forgot! I need to talk to you some more about
> the night of that party. You're the last one. I'll
> be at the station in about 30. Can I call you back
> then?

Forgot! I need to talk to you some more about the night of that party. You're the last one. I'll be at the station in about 30. Can I call you back then?

Oh, no. My heart began to hammer inside my chest. He'd be asking about what interactions of Mil's I'd witnessed. I swallowed though a lump in my throat that felt as big as a golf ball, then forced myself to take deep breaths, though each filled me with no more air than if I'd been taking it in through a straw.

Despite everything, I had to get going with my day. I went into the bedroom I'd had converted into a closet with full-length mirrors, custom cabinets and lighting that mimicked daylight. I could see myself as clearly as if standing out in the sun.

I chose black leggings to wear with a Chanel cashmere tunic—from my store, of course. Added my favorite black patent leather Jimmy Choo booties with the partial gold metallic heel and ... oh, it meant having to take a cab or Uber to work. Because who wanted to wear these shoes on cobblestones, which, under my feet, were like mini mountains to overcome, at least in heels? No, I'd wear my Gucci flats and carry the booties with me. There. Done.

Now ready and happy about my choice of outfit, I headed to work.

Just as I unlocked the door to my shop, Denise Bouchard waved at me from the order counter at the coffee kiosk on the other side of the courtyard.

Seeing her reminded me that Amelia had said something at *comida* about her, and that it had bugged me, much like an itch impossible to scratch without help.

"Oh, hey, Carli, I'm coming over. Leave the door unlocked, please!" She called out. Her voice echoed in the near-empty courtyard, slicing through the morning air.

I needed to go through the usual opening routine with the lights, world music, vanilla and lavender-scented candles, and making sure no garments lay about where they shouldn't be, but she could come now.

"Sure, lock up behind you!"

She gave me a thumbs up.

I recalled that Amelia had told me that she'd been put off by Denise's rudeness to the waitstaff at the party. Something about that comment irritated me like a small stone in stiletto-heeled shoes digging into the foot while the wearer tries to make it look effortless to walk in the things. Because, as far as I knew, that didn't match up to the Denise I knew.

I'd ask her about the party, try to get some information about that glass of wine.

"Carli, did you hear me?" Said Denise, bringing me back to the present. She looked at me, her eyes piercing through my thoughts.

I hadn't heard her come in.

"Oh, Denise ... huh ... I'm ... I'm sorry. Just spacing out over here a little." I smiled at her. "What was it you said? I promise to listen this time." A mirror would have reflected a red face at me, giving me the look of a ripe tomato, no doubt.

"Spacing out about what? A new man in your life, maybe?" She said, grinning with her whole face.

Despite the smile, I sensed nervous energy coming from her, the way we could feel storms approaching because of static electricity in the air, something I rarely sensed from her. I blamed it on all the goings-on of the past few days for sending me into paranoia-land.

But also, why did it seem like the whole town wanted to see me with a man? They didn't ask men such questions, did they?

Questions as probing as a dentist's metal instrument in the mouth? "No, nothing like that. I'm married already," I replied.

"What?!" Replied Denise, her eyebrows up to her hairline, glancing around as if a husband might materialize in front of us.

"To this shop!" I said, then laughed, realizing how my answer could have shocked her.

"Oh, phew! I wondered how I'd missed out on that piece of news!" She exclaimed with a smile that made it to her eyes. Relief washed over her face that she hadn't somehow lost something.

"Did you enjoy the concert the other night? And the party?"

The air between us changed as if the sun had slipped behind a cloud.

Her face dropped, and she turned away from me like she didn't want me to see.

Well, that was interesting ...

By then, I'd unlocked the door and flipped the sign to Open. Barely a minute had passed when the door chime tinkled, announcing the start of the business day for me. We both turned that way. A woman came in, followed by two others.

"Hola, welcome. Let me know if you have questions," I called to them. They thanked me, and the three of them seemed to continue a conversation they had clearly started before coming in.

"So, what was it I missed when you came in?"

"I was saying ..." she started, then took a deep breath. "Hmm ... that candle smells so nice. Vanilla?"

"Yes!" Her comment made me smile. I loved it when customers mentioned the small touches I loved adding. It meant they noticed.

"We're going to the city. Mexico, I mean," she continued. "The Four Seasons—a formal wedding in mid-November. I'm hoping you have something, designer, that doesn't cost too much because I'm not likely to wear it again. These things always have the same guests, you know, so ..." Her words tumbled over one another.

"Of course."

This sort of dilemma was like solving a Rubik's Cube to me, and I was lightning fast and good at it.

A Theia smoky blue formal dress in the small area I reserved for formal wear was perfect for her. I'd guide her to choose it because she'd look elegant and fashionable in it.

"I might have something. Let's take a look."

"Ooh, great!"

We got to the rack, and I pulled out the Theia, a stunning gown. Smoky blue, with 3D embroidery just a shade lighter than the dress itself through the entire gown, even over the sheer shoulders and sleeves. A masterpiece! Its color complimented Denise's dark hair and matched her blue eyes as if made for her alone. I wanted to see her in it now!

"It just needs to be taken in a little at the hips and hemmed up two inches. Lucky you!" I said, allowing the silk fabric to slip through my fingers like water, both of us admiring it.

"And the sleeve length is perfect for you to show off one of your beautiful chunky bracelets. That's all the jewelry this dress needs." I glanced at her wrist, picturing a wide, intricately carved silver piece I'd seen on her wrist before.

As I helped her get into the gown, I tried bringing up Mil and the party again.

Immediately, Denise stiffened, reminding me of Dap puffing up his fur when he perceived a threat. She changed the subject, and each time I circled back to it, I mostly got a one-word answer before she changed it again, so I let it go.

I didn't want to spook her, yet her reaction set off alarm bells in my head. It felt like catching a glimpse behind a curtain—straining to see what was concealed there, yet finding everything shrouded in shadows, illuminated only by a few specks of light.

Denise and her husband had been sitting at *that* table, and the thought felt like a splinter under the skin.

Josefina, my head seamstress, arrived at the shop to pin the gown, and the whole time Denise seemed out of sorts, her excitement over the Mexico City event drained away like sand through an hourglass. She clearly couldn't wait to leave my shop.

I had been dying to ask her about the table seating. Yet, given her current mood, the question would stick out like a cactus in a rose garden, and with the way she was behaving, I didn't dare.

Amy's U.S. phone number, that's what I needed. I'd have to either dig it up—or wait until she returned on Friday.

Desperate to pivot the conversation to another subject, I asked about Bill. I hoped she'd say something about what Lisa had told me because, of course, I was curious. And what if it had something to do with the wine?

I shook the thought away. The poor woman had enough to do dealing with him and his medications without me prying, and I didn't want to add another helping of stress on her plate. And to bring that up, I'd have to tell her what Lisa told me. She'd be hurt that her friend babbled about her secrets.

Could I somehow let her know her friend wasn't worthy of her secrets without saying her friend wasn't worthy of her secrets? I sighed silently. No. I would then feel the consequences of being the messenger of bad news.

Finally, she paid for the dress and left.

I gazed at her as she hesitated just outside the door, as though she were at a crossroads. She nearly turned toward the coffee cart, but changed her mind and headed to the street instead.

What secret was Denise keeping? All this worry coming from her wasn't like the Denise I knew. It was as if I'd opened the cover of a book, only to discover that the story inside no longer matched its cover.

Though she'd disappeared at least a full minute before, I kept staring out the door, a thought forming in my mind, one misted over as if by an early morning fog behind which something hides, something you *know* is there, but can't see. Won't see until the fog lifts.

Before the metaphorical fog could dissipate and show me the secret hiding behind it, however, my phone rang, which made the thought scatter like autumn leaves hit by a gust of wind.

My eyes bugged out. I feared looking at the display and seeing Antonio's name there, him ready to question me about who Mil had spoken to, who might have given her a glass of wine ...

But, no, it was Manuel, and a rush of relief like that of stepping into an air-conditioned space on a sweltering day came over me.

CHAPTER 18

I answered the phone. "¡*Hola, Primo*!"

"¡*Hola*, cousin!" He exclaimed in return, his voice rising on the last syllable.

"I have a funny story for you, but first, I saw Liam go into the Coldwell Banker office this morning." Said Manuel, his voice sounding like he was in a hurry to get somewhere.

"Really? Isn't it too soon? Mil isn't even back from the ... well, you know." I hated to say the word morgue. So gruesome. "It's only been a few days!" I heard my own voice quivering.

"That's what I'm thinking, but he probably just wants someone to look at the house and tell him what he needs to do to it, so he can sell it when the time comes. And he might want to sell quickly. It's not his home, just his mother's." Manuel replied, his words still coming fast.

I caught unease in his voice as if he was using this story to distract me, or as if he'd just called with that as a pretext, hoping I'd tell him something new, without him having to ask.

"Yes. I can see that. His life *is* in Dallas. Plus, without her here, he doesn't have much to do."

I sighed. Mil's whole world erased, like a sandcastle swept away by a rogue wave. Someone would buy her house. It would sell in no time because she had updated it with every available luxury. They'd then proceed with obliterating every trace of Mil out of it.

Something was definitely off in Manuel's way of talking, though. Besides speaking quickly, for him, I detected a hint of hesitation, like an actor forgetting his lines mid-performance.

It irked me that he hadn't told me about the note becoming due next month. Between that and the wine, what was I supposed to think? Even if this was Manuel, someone I'd never have thought capable of murder. Before now.

Should I ask him about it? Share my suspicions about Janice?

"Manuel?" I asked.

"*¿Mande?*"

I looked at the wall clock. "Can you be at El Café at eleven fifteen?"

"But I'll see you tomorrow night, right? Dinner with Antonio and his new lady?" He asked, sounding surprised I wanted to see him now, too.

"Yes, but this can't wait, and I don't want Antonio to hear."

"You ... you don't want Antonio to hear?" He hesitated, as if unsure how to take this in. I remained silent.

"Bueno, Carli, okay." He finally added, a hint of resignation in his voice.

We'd never kept secrets like this from Antonio. The weight of my words felt like stones in my pocket. But I could tell Manuel also saw the necessity now, just like I did. I might have wanted to talk about him giving Mil the wine that might have killed her. And best to not talk about that over the phone.

As soon as Sofia arrived at work—ten minutes late, average for her—I flew out the door, and walked down Canal Street to El Café. This being late morning and near lunchtime, there were many people to skirt by on the narrow sidewalk as I made my way.

Manuel arrived at the same time and held the door open for me. Because of the narrow doorway, my arm brushed against his torso as I entered, but as usual around him, I ignored my body's reaction. My traitorous body that wanted to get even closer. And linger. *Despite* the fact he might have committed murder. I felt like a vine wrapped around itself, twisted and uncertain, my emotions tangled in doubt and desire.

We placed our orders and agreed to sit at an inside table. There were few people and the café's music should muffle our conversation enough.

As soon as we sat, he started in.

"You won't believe ..." He began, but I cut him off.

"No, me first. *¡Muy importante!*"

My words came out sharper than I'd intended.

Surprised at my rude interruption, he put out both hands in a gesture of capitulation, a bit of a smirk on his face.

"Manuel, about that wine you gave to Mil. Do you remember anything odd about it?"

His eyes widened, and he seemed to choke on his words. "Odd? How? It was just wine, Carli—how could I have known something else might be in it?" He'd been quick to wave it off.

"You sure? It's just ..." I trailed off, watching him closely.

Something in his reaction was off kilter, like a painting hanging slightly askew on a wall. The Manuel I knew was always so confident, but now there was a flicker of doubt in his eyes. I might not even have picked up on this except that I knew him so well.

"I'm sure, Carlita. Can we talk about something else? This whole thing with Mil will be resolved by Antonio and his team. There's nothing for *us* to do." He casually moved his index finger in the air between us, indicating and emphasizing we were the "us" he meant.

He looked at me with narrowed eyes, speculation shining from them. I could tell he was thinking about what had happened in New York, and probably wondering if I was doing it again. Getting involved in a murder investigation, that is.

Then he forced a smile, his shoulders tense like coiled springs. He took a sip of his coffee.

I was walking a tightrope, my emotions pulling me in different directions, like the north and south poles of a magnet. But I wanted to tell him about Janice. That's why I'd wanted to meet.

Because despite my suspicions about Manuel, part of me wanted to confide in him, perhaps out of habit. Perhaps because I wanted to pretend to myself that I didn't suspect him?

Either way, I needed help to decide how to tell Antonio about her, about the letter. Right now, if I took Manuel out of the equation, Janice was my most likely suspect. And Antonio knew nothing about it! I cringed at what he might do once he discovered I had taken it ...

To the background of reggae music, the bassline thumping like a heartbeat, I told him about the letter, that if Millicent Jones died, Janice wouldn't have to pay her debt back.

"And how did you see this letter?" He asked, his voice tinged with a gravelly undertone, brows furrowed, thunder in his eyes.

"What does it matter?" I asked, my voice rising like boiling water about to spill over the pot.

"Did you want to know or not? It makes her look very suspicious!" I exclaimed, not willing to tell him I'd entered her house without her permission. My heart pounded in my chest.

"Carlita," he sighed, dragging my name, reaching across the table with his hands, seeking mine.

I looked at his beautiful hands—beautiful despite the knicks and rough spots from spending so much time in a kitchen using dangerous knives—as if they held answers.

After a moment's hesitation, I reached out with my own. He gently took them, his warm grip enveloping mine, the heat seeping down to my bones.

"I went to her house. Because I suspect her, okay? We have to figure out who did this. I ... I worry you'll be blamed, Manuel." I said this last in a near whisper, breath shaky.

His eyes widened, a flicker of something unreadable passing through them.

"You were in her *house*?" He asked, his face now blank, unreadable.

I nodded.

"And ... Janice. She was there?" he added.

I blanched, but told him the truth despite my pounding heart. "No, Manuel, no. She wasn't there. You see, I have a key ..."

He interrupted me. "Carlita! *What* are you doing? You can't be involved in this."

He yanked his hands away from mine, and it felt like large band-aids were being torn off my skin.

I said nothing, using my eyes to plead silently with him. Did he not understand I was only trying to save him?

"We *need* to find out who did this. And she's acting strangely. I think she did it."

He stared at me, apparently having no words to express how he felt about me breaking into Janice's house. He shook his head in disappointment. We sat across from one another, both silent. Both waiting on the other to speak first.

Finally, clearly having decided to ignore my actions for now—he knew how stubborn I could be—he said, "I wonder if Antonio knows. I think they questioned her. Maybe they searched her house, too."

The thing was that Antonio couldn't know about the letter ... if he'd searched her house before I got there, he'd have taken it as the strong evidence it was.

Her house hadn't looked like it had been searched by the police. And wouldn't she have been talking about a search with whomever she had been on the phone with when I sneaked back out? Though I couldn't hear all that she'd said, there'd been no apprehension in her voice.

Now, unless I told him, Antonio would never know about the letter since I'd taken it with me ...

No way could I tell Manuel this part. A prickle of sweat formed on the back of my neck. He'd make me go to Antonio this instant. With the letter.

My breath hitched at the thought that I was withholding evidence in a murder investigation.

Manuel assumed that Antonio would find the letter if he hadn't already. Why would he think that I'd take it, knowing how important it could become to the case? Antonio's case. Not mine.

To change the conversation, I spoke first.

"So, what story did you want to tell me?"

He shrugged as if it were no longer important.

"Come on. You said it was funny. I could use a laugh."

"Well, I'm not in a laughing mood anymore, Carli." He looked at me intently.

"Please, we'll both laugh, and then we'll go back to our work and feel better."

Shrugging, he half-heartedly told me the story. "Just one of those Hollywood stars came to the restaurant last night," he started, air-quoting "Hollywood star."

"Oh, yeah, who?" I asked, finding myself curious.

"Leon Grand. Acted like a jerk at first, but then he invited people who were waiting in line to join him for dinner, and he covered the whole check."

"Alright!" I said, offering him my hand in a high-five, and he returned the gesture, a half-smile on his face. He was beginning to forgive me.

"And because he ordered all the best of the best and ten times over, that check is paying the restaurant's rent for the next two weeks!" He lifted his coffee cup as if making a toast.

I was smiling wide by then, happy for him, and imagining the scene.

"It's nice to see you smile, Manuel," I added, realizing that despite my confession, the smile I knew so well was beginning to show, like the sun coming out after days of rain.

His features closed back up at my words, and I cursed myself. I'd blown his good mood.

I covered his right hand with my left and squeezed.

We finished our drinks and left, agreeing that he would come to me tomorrow evening and we'd walk to dinner together.

I followed Calle Canal back to my shop, the sun above, warm and bright. Happy faces buzzed up and down the street, tourists, and locals, usually a sight that lifted me, but today, it didn't hit the same.

What was Manuel hiding, if anything? More importantly, what was I willing to do to find out?

Every glance he threw me, every hesitation before speaking
...

Would we find out at dinner tomorrow whether the lab results
were back from the morgue?

Because then, we'd know if Mil had been poisoned by the
wine Manuel gave her.

Chapter 19

On the spur of the moment, I walked right past my shop and headed toward home instead. Thinking would be difficult with customers coming and going and Sofia's constant chatter about everything under the sun.

Sofia seemed to love the sound of her own voice, a constant melody in the shop. But customers ate it up, especially tourists who loved her local tales. Sales spiked when she was around, so I let her be.

At home, I grabbed a bottle of cool water from my fridge and flopped down on the couch, letting out a deep, lung-emptying sigh.

Dap jumped on my lap, and, pulling him closer, I buried myself in his neck, his fur soft against my face. One loud, offended meow later, I pulled my head back and simply petted him.

He sat, rigid, on guard for a moment, as if waiting for the next "blow," then relaxed, but only so much. I knew better. Nuzzles were to be given on his terms only. I chuckled softly, and he turned away but sank more comfortably into my lap, purring like an idling truck engine. I rolled my eyes, grinning widely.

A thought pushed through me. Amy! I had to find her U.S. phone number. I jerked and my reaction startled Dap. Flattening his ears, he shot me a look of irritation, hopped off the couch, and settled onto a side chair just as I stood.

"Sorry, Dap!" I exclaimed, as I rushed toward my home office, as if propelled there by a tornado, anxious to solve this thing once and for all.

I dug around my desk drawers, the rustle of old papers filling the room. No luck. It should have been in the Contacts on my phone, but no, I only had her San Miguel number. Why hadn't I added it in there to begin with? *Idiota*—idiot, I chided myself and shook my head.

Back in the kitchen, I stood at the window. The sway of the tall bamboo in the neighbor's garden caught my eye. Was I going to stand here and watch it grow?

Enough. I grabbed my bag and headed back to work.

The shop was bustling when I got there. Sofia shot me a grateful smile, her eyes shining. Five or six women browsed, arms loaded with treasures. Two stood at the register and I hurried to help. As soon as they left, my phone rang. Manuel. Now what?

"Hey, Manuel." I answered.

"I was walking to the bank after we met up and saw Liam going into the station."

Confused for a moment, I asked: "What station?"

"*¿Mande?* What station? The *police* station! What other one would I be talking about?"

"Well, the bus station?" I asked, hesitant, realizing that Liam wasn't likely to take a bus. Hiring a car to go to wherever was more his style.

He ignored me and continued. "Antonio must have called him in."

"*Reeeally?* Now, *that's* interesting?" I stood in the middle of an aisle, holding a dress on a hanger, staring at nothing.

My mind raced. "So, do you think they suspect the death wasn't natural?"

He paused. "I don't know. Could be they got the autopsy back. Or they've come across new information."

"Oh ..." I slapped a hand over my mouth, my heart beating on my breastbone as if trying to escape. What might the report say? Soon, I realized, we'd know what had killed her.

Sofia, done at the register, and on the other side of the shop taking clothes out of the changing rooms to put back on the racks, shot me a curious glance, her eyes like small searchlights. I turned away. Not ready to say anything to her, or anyone else.

I noticed a burned-out candle at the end of the register counter. With the phone in the crook of my neck, I pulled a new gardenia scented candle from a shelf under the register and lit it, mesmerized, for a moment, by the flicker of the flame. I breathed in its floral scent and smiled. Little things like this made me so happy, no matter the other things happening around me.

"It will be alright, Carlita." Said Manuel.

"Antonio didn't say anything to you?"

"He doesn't owe me that, *Prima*. I told you." He sounded annoyed with me, his voice tense, a tight string ready to snap.

"I know, but, well, you could ask. *Sí?* He still tells you *some* things about his cases, right? Why not just ask if he got the autopsy report, or if he called Liam in for other reasons?"

Manuel sighed, his heavy exhale traveling along the phone line, as if releasing a burden.

"He shares stuff about some of his cases some of the time. But usually *he* brings it up. And it's not usually about people in my life, and didn't happen right after I've seen them, and given them ..." He trailed off with a sigh.

A scratchy feeling developed in my throat. "I'll ask him at dinner tomorrow."

Manuel hesitated. "Might not be a good idea with his new girlfriend there."

An awkward silence stretched between us.

The air in the bubble of us on the phone together thickened.

"Why can't you call him and tell him the truth?" A pause on the other end made me realize what I'd just said. That I thought Manuel was hiding things.

"I mean, that you saw Liam go into the station and wondered why," I added, heat rising to my cheeks.

"I suppose I could," he said with no conviction.

A huge sigh escaped me.

"What?" He asked.

"Manuel ... why not tell Antonio about the glass of wine? He'd never think you'd do something like that, right?"

"Not that easy. The cop in him will have to bring me in for questioning, no matter what he thinks. The prosecutor would expect him to. And you too, because you saw me give it to her."

"Oh ... *sí* ... I guess you're right."

"Hopefully, he finds who did this before I have to tell him anything at all."

I gripped the phone tighter.

My mind raced. Manuel could be in big trouble. If I knew for certain he'd done it, would I tell? I shook the thought away, a dog shaking off water.

"How do I tell him about Janice without causing a scene?" I asked, steering the conversation away from his actions.

All this cloak and dagger stuff. Life had been so beautiful and good four days ago. My biggest problem had been to escape the social gathering outside the theater to sneak off to change Manuel's place card. My eyes teared at the simplicity of that evening. Now?

The stifling atmosphere of the shop pressed on me. I needed to be on my couch with Dap. "Sofia, I'm going home for *comida*. Remember to lock up when you go, okay?"

She looked up and grinned, her face a splash of sunshine. "*Ciao, bella!*"

I'd nearly reached the door when it opened, and a man walked in. A tall, sandy-haired man with tired eyes and a drawn face, an aura of dejection all around him.

Chapter 20

"**H**eaded somewhere?" Asked the man, a subtle whiff of his cologne reaching me as he glanced at the Louis Vuitton Monogram tote draped over my arm.

Maybe because Manuel had told me he'd seen him go into the police station, seeing him here shocked me, but I recouped.

"Liam! Hello, welcome. Going home for *comida*, that's all." My voice sounded high-pitched even to me, and he narrowed his eyes ever so slightly.

"Oh, sorry. Do you have a minute? I won't keep you long," he said, attempting a smile while scratching the back of his head, his eyes roaming the shop.

My shoulders sagged. "Sure, how can I help?"

"I wondered about all of Mom's stuff, her clothes, you know." His gaze continued its trek around the store as if he wondered whether this was the right place for Mil's stuff, before settling back on mine.

"The furniture, too," he added, apparently an afterthought.

He locked eyes with me as if gauging my sincerity.

"Do you want to consign some of it?"

"Not sure yet. I think so. How does that work, exactly? I talked to a realtor, and she said it would be best if all of mom's stuff was gone before I put the house on the market."

Then, seeming to think that he needed to explain himself, he added, "I need to take care of some of these things now. As soon as I can have the memorial service, I have to go back to Dallas because of work issues. I hadn't planned on ..." He shrugged his shoulders, then tried again. "I hadn't planned on ... on this when I came over and I left many things hanging." He looked morose.

"Oh, of course, I understand. Well, as far as the clothes, you bring them here," I gestured towards the racks of dresses, shirts, pants, and skirts, "and we discuss how much for each piece. Or, if there's a lot of them, you leave it for me to price, and you come back later and say if you're okay with those prices."

With a large amount of clothing, I usually went to the customer's home, and we went over it all there. But with all my ambivalent feelings regarding Liam, I thought it best if he brought everything here.

Except Liam seemed to be one step ahead of me.

"Oh, what if, well, can you come to the house and look through it all?" He hesitated before asking, rubbing at his temple as if grappling with a heavy decision, or expected to be denied.

His request hung in the air, thickening the atmosphere between us, until I finally found my voice again. Well, at least, partially.

"Uh, I ... don't, I ..." I could now add blabbering *idiota* to my list of skills.

He frowned at me, confusion in his eyes.

My professional self took over, *gracias a dio*. I took a deep breath to steady myself.

After all, the fact that he was here in my shop meant Antonio hadn't arrested him, so it must have been a routine visit to the police station.

"Sorry, Liam, sure I can do that, but not for a couple of days, I don't think." I transferred my tote to my other shoulder. "I'm behind on things here. Also, your mom had a lot of good designer clothes and I'll have to research some of them. Meanwhile, you could bring a few pieces in if you want an idea."

"Hmmm ..." He said, glancing around again while running his hands down the sides of his pants, as if to wipe sweat off them.

I tilted my head, watching him closely. Were sweaty hands normal for him?

Red-rimmed eyes, sweaty hands, gauntness? Grief? We all handled it differently. That's all this was, I decided. It didn't fit what I knew of him, but the man's mother had just died unexpectedly. Of course, he wasn't himself.

Maybe I could go sort through what was surely an amazing inventory, recalling the clothes Mil usually wore. A lot of my clientele was old enough to appreciate her style, plus she dressed younger than you'd expect.

"Well, you know, I can go to you. Can I call you about it later? What's your number?" I asked, fumbling around in my tote to pull my phone from the inside pocket.

He recited it, and I entered it into my Contacts.

"And what's your number?" he then asked.

Twirling a strand of my hair around a finger, I shared the numbers for the store and my cell phone.

"Alright, thanks, Carli," he said, managing a thin smile that didn't erase the sadness in his eyes.

After he left, the wind chime over the door tinkling behind him, I stood there, staring at the door, feeling badly for him. If Mamá died, how would I be? How would I react?

Soon, thoughts of Manuel quickly superseded Liam Jones. He still had said nothing to me about that danged note.

It made no sense, considering we knew one another's deeper secrets, even. I feared for him, for what would happen once this was found out ... I meant *if* he was found out.

"You okay, Carli?" A small voice said behind me. Sofia had noticed my somewhat out of character behavior with Liam. Her voice showed concern.

I'd normally have jumped at the opportunity to go check out all those designer clothes and furniture. Today.

"Sí, Sofia, *gracias*." I switched the tote to my other shoulder again. "I'm thinking about how to accommodate all of Mil's stuff in here."

"What about the back storage?" She asked.

"Yes, but I want to look at the clothes before putting them in there. I guess it will be best to go to the house and look at everything first. She has—had—really nice quality clothes. And a lot of them."

"Oh, okay," Sofia replied.

To change the subject, I said, "well, might as well leave together. It's *comida* time for sure now." I managed a smile for her.

"Alright, you're the *jefa*," she said, grinning now. She walked to the register counter and unlocked the metal drawer where we kept our handbags and pulled hers out, shutting it again to a satisfying whoosh.

We left but not until I dropped the bomb that I wouldn't be coming back this afternoon, another strange thing for me to do. especially on a Monday. She knew I loved the slowness of Monday afternoons to cull the racks. But she didn't probe, and for that, I silently thanked her.

Once home, allowing the familiar scent of the aromatic candles I often burned to envelop me, I headed straight to the kettle, of course.

"Dapperoo! Mamá's home." I called out as usual.

Tea now ready, I sat on the couch, and Dap jumped up and sat straight up next to me, his front paws touching my leg, staring into my eyes. *What was that about?* I found it difficult to relax with him so wound up. I stroked his back in an attempt to calm us both.

I took a sip of matcha, its warmth filling me but failing to calm my mind.

Amy! It all revolved around that danged seating plan. So hard to tell who had been meant to sit at that table. So many switched seats all the time, place cards ignored. I should know. It could still help, a place to start.

I headed to my office once more, my kitten heels (Prada padded leather sling back pumps) tapping against the tile floor. On the way, I dialed her Mexico number from my cell, hoping she'd come back early, hoping she'd changed her greeting to include her U.S. number, but no.

It was the same as before. "*Hola*, it's Amy. We're in Dallas 'til Friday. Leave a message!"

The silence after the voicemail beep was like a vacuum, sucking in all my frustrations. I left a message. Again.

I leaned against the doorframe to my office, asking the room where the danged phone number might be. Suddenly, an epiphany nearly knocked me off my feet.

Buen dios, Carlota Maria Garcia Cano, where is your mind?!

I sighed big, my eyes to the ceiling, my head shaking back and forth.

I dialed a number I knew well, and threw myself back into my office chair, a nice Herman Miller someone had brought in a couple of years back, the most comfortable office chair ever. Never heard a creak out of this thing.

The ring tone played twice, three times, each ring elongating time, and I nearly gave up. Just the woman I wanted to talk to picked up on the fourth ring, and I breathed a sigh of relief.

"Hola, so nice to hear your voice, Juana!" I said.

She hesitated until she recognized me, a moment of silence suspended between us.

"Oh, Carli? Of course, it's you. Sorry, I was distracted by some paperwork."

A light rustle of papers from her end made her statement more tangible.

"That's okay. *Trabajar*, we all have to do it." Work, of course. I smiled.

The sound of someone typing on a keyboard, probably her, punctuated my statement. Juana worked hard to keep Música Clásica Esencial on its feet and the operation running smoothly.

"How's the family?" I asked her.

The tapping stopped.

"Oh, *muy bien*, thank you for asking. How about you? How's your aunt doing, do you know?"

The tension in my shoulders eased some.

"She's fine now, *gracias*. False alarm."

I twirled hair around my finger, a way to slow me down and not jump ahead. This was Mexico, and social niceties had to be respected before any request for help.

"Ah, *bueno*. Good. I hope it all works out for you and your family, then."

I couldn't help my fingers tapping on my desk.

"Thank you, Juana. You are so kind." Now impatient with the small talk, I jumped right in.

"Listen, do you have Amy's U.S. cell phone number? It's some place in my home office, but not sure under what it's buried. I need to call her."

"Oh, sure. I don't think she'll mind me giving it to you," she said.

I rolled my eyes. Amy and my mom were close friends. *I* was even close friends with her, even though she always tried to set me up with her latest favorite bachelor—conspiring with my mother. Of course, Juana felt it appropriate to give me her number.

"Here you go. Do you have a pen and paper?" Asked Juana.

I bit my lower lip, struggling to hold back my impatience. Juana did not understand the urgency of things, after all.

"Yes," I wanted to scream, but said it like a normal woman would, proud of my self-control.

The pen slid smoothly along the paper as I scribbled down the number. I said goodbye and hung up as soon as socially acceptable.

Just as I began to save the number in my Contacts, my phone rang and startled me, sending shivers down my spine. I let out a short half-swallowed scream like a character in a horror movie who doesn't want the attacker in the next room to hear her. On some level, I realized I'd been drinking too much green tea.

I rolled my eyes at myself, feeling foolish, when I saw it was Esme. They say imagination will get you everywhere, but in my case, imagination often took me down roads it had no business traveling. Wrong roads, fake roads, weird roads.

As if by design, as soon as I hung up with her—and before I could dial Amy's number—a text came in.

> Can you talk?

The soft light from the text message demanded my immediate attention. But at the same time, a call came in ...

Manuel. I stared at the phone's display for a moment. He sure was calling me a lot today. Guilt? Fear? Just nervous?

My thumb hovered over the keyboard, hesitating.

CHAPTER 21

The sun shone brightly the next morning, the bougainvillea on my roof terrace bloomed to bursting, the songs of birds filled the house through all the living, dining, and kitchen windows I'd opened, the doors to the terrace attached to my living room thrown wide open. There. Perhaps the pall setting over my home because of the events surrounding Mil's death would now clear out?

I sank into the couch, holding a cup of matcha at my lips, the earthy aroma filling my nostrils, hair disheveled, Dap next to me, lounging like a proper Roaring Twenties gentleman, his front legs stretched out, white paws kneading the side of my thigh; his go-to-move when he sensed a dark mood he didn't understand. And goodness, he'd sensed a lot of that lately.

But why did this mood persist? I wondered. After all, we'd discovered that Manuel hadn't done it, *Right Dap?* I stroked his soft fur, a tiny smile curving my lips.

• • • ● ● • ● ● • •

Manuel had come over in the late afternoon yesterday, so we could sit on the rooftop and watch the sunset while we shared a bottle of Bordeaux wine he'd brought over. He realized that his interaction with Mil the night of the Música Clásica Esencial party upset me, that the worry was still with me.

Oh, if you only knew the extent of it, I thought.

A woman from the expat community dead under suspicious circumstances, something that could affect our businesses. And Manuel having handed her a glass of wine that might have killed her.

He'd apologized for not spending more than a few minutes at a time in a coffee shop with me the past few days, knowing how upset I was about Mil, the wine, and him.

I was soon chastened for even thinking he might have done Mil in. Because, quite casually, he'd come clean.

He'd told me he'd wondered what to do about a note coming due on Mil's investment. She'd talked about renewing it to keep earning on the restaurant, but he wanted to pay it all back, wanted to get out from under the debt as soon as possible.

But with her dead, he worried about the police thinking he'd killed her in an attempt to avoid paying it back, especially if anything were found in the wine she'd drunk.

He reminded me that his connection to Antonio, and the fact he'd been a cop, would not help him, but probably make it worse. The prosecutor wouldn't want it to look like these things would let him get away with murder and would try even harder to convict him, even if only the smallest amount of evidence could be found, even if it was all only circumstantial.

He had no idea how Liam might want to proceed. So much had been going on that he hadn't taken the time to bring up having a meeting to discuss it with him.

Finally, he asked my opinion, his eyes seeking mine as if hunting for an anchor.

He had the money!

Instead of giving him my opinion on what the should do, I'd taken a deep breath and dived into the deep. I told him my suspicions that he might have done it. Killed Millicent Jones.

That I thought he might not have the money to repay her, that I saw she made him crazy, always trying to tell him how to run his business, about the expected free meals and bottles of wine. And about the "*I* own this restaurant, you know. I own him, you know," she threw around all the time.

That *Papá* told me on Sunday about one of the notes coming due next month, and not knowing if he had the money, I assumed the worst. Because he'd said nothing to me about it and didn't we always tell one another these things?

Told him I thought he'd rather kill someone than ask his father to help him repay that loan.

"*¿Qué!?*" He asked, his disbelief filling the space between us, spitting out wine. Luckily, we'd been on the roof, and he'd spit out far enough to miss some falling on, and staining, his white shirt.

He stared at me for at least a full five seconds without saying a word, his eyes wide open, his mouth ajar. Not a good look on him.

A distinct and palpable electric charge sizzled between us.

I stared back, my face getting redder by the second, a heat to rival that of the sun rising to my face, because, of course, as soon as I'd said it all, everything bursting out of me like champagne out of a bottle at New Year's, I realized how ridiculous it sounded.

Manuel laughed.

At first a slow rumble, then an escalation like piano keys played faster and faster, the melody dancing through the air until the sound of each one crashed into the other at high speed. He managed to put his glass of wine down on the table next to his chair. Then laughed harder until it morphed into a cough, scratching at the still evening air.

Meanwhile, the sun sank lower in the sky, and the city's sounds enveloped us, normal everyday occurrences. The ordinary backdrop stood in stark contrast to the extraordinary accusation I had almost flung at him.

By the time he slowed, I also shook with laughter, but with my mouth closed. I felt buoyant, and ashamed, and silly, and oh, so ecstatic.

I'd been wrong!

"You *really* believed that, Carlita?"

He looked at me as though he'd never seen me, his eyes open even wider, mouth still hanging down, breathing from it in spurts like panting bursts of air, like he was doing his best to not start laughing again. Tears of mirth escaped from the corners of his eyes, and yes, one rolled down his right cheek. He wiped at it, and in doing so, lost control, and burst out anew.

With my face still burning like a furnace against the cool evening air, I shrugged my shoulders and offered him a small, sheepish smile. My body kept on quivering with silent laughter, giddy with relief.

He'd shaken his head, the motion vigorous and insistent, a few times. He'd then stood up, put out his hand for me to stand too, which I'd done. And still chuckling, he'd enveloped me in a huge hug, his arms creating a warm, secure fortress around me One I never wanted to leave ...

As ecstatic as my discovery of his innocence had made me, this morning, the mood I'd been in when I'd thought he'd done it came crawling back.

Despite finding out he wasn't guilty, a nagging itch of curiosity and concern prevailed in me.

I still wanted to find out who killed a woman who shopped in my store, who lived in my town, who ran in my mother's circle. Plus, I had that letter no one but Manuel and I knew about ...

Plus, just because I believed Manuel, who's to say some cop on the force might not? Antonio wasn't the only one to decide who got arrested and who didn't. The unease settled in my stomach like a stone. He had a boss too. The prosecutor.

Antonio, as the detective sergeant—simply followed the prosecutor's orders. It wouldn't be his call whether to question and arrest Manuel. If it came to that, he'd likely be in the dark until after the questioning, or even an arrest, took place.

Either way, gossip spread like wildfire in this town. Manuel could go from restaurateur to pariah overnight. Imagine a restaurant where the owner is on the list of suspects for a murder. Not good for business, that.

So, to ensure he didn't get accused to begin with, and to assure the guilty party got what he or she deserved, a new determination to get to the truth lit up like a fire within me.

I stood, stretched my arms up as far as I could, and bent back a little, hoping the stretch would clear my head and unkink my limbs. Well, what next? Dap wasn't coming up with answers. I wasn't coming up with answers. Yet.

My whole house seemed to hold its breath.

Who could have wanted Mil dead? Besides Janice? Because one letter did not mean for certain that she'd killed her, and she couldn't get convicted with just that. Right?

Also, later last night, Antonio had told Manuel that the medical examiner was now certain Mil had died from something she'd ingested. He just didn't know what yet.

Whether she'd overdosed or been given something, they didn't yet know that either. But they'd found several drugs in her system.

Manuel and I and, though he wouldn't say, Antonio, now believed that Mil *had* been killed.

CHAPTER 22

No way had she been prescribed medications that, in combination, could kill her. Her Dallas doctor would surely soon confirm. This might mean someone gave her drugs she shouldn't have been taking. Which still pointed to the glass of wine Manuel had handed her.

The morning air chilled my skin as I walked to the shop, where the door creaked open—the hinges needed oiling—and the tinkle of the wind chime and the familiar scent of gardenia and other florals welcomed me. Even the clothes on the racks seemed to be saying hello. I know, silly me.

The lights flickered to life, and I did the usual opening stuff. Dealt with customers after opening. Spoke to Sofia about coming in two more mornings per week, making it five instead of three. To my surprise, she loved the idea. Her eyes sparkled, excited.

"Yes, I have time," she said, flipping through a textbook she had placed on the counter, "if I can study a bit between customers." Fine by me.

The cash register's chime punctuated each transaction, but the whole time, my mind was on Mil's death, killings in general, murders! Gosh, I hated those words.

Just before *comida*, to my surprise, the soft sound of the door chimes announced the arrival of Manuel and Antonio. I looked at them, so out of place here. All this frilly stuff wasn't their thing unless they were admiring it on the body of a beautiful woman, so no way were they here to shop.

They had hardly stepped foot in the place since the opening. On a very few occasions, Manuel had dropped by, yes, but not Antonio. He'd helped with painting, and at that, two days only, but that was it.

"¡Hola Prima!" Said Manuel. His deep voice cut through the quiet shop.

"¡Hola, Prima!" Parroted Antonio, running his fingers through scarves displayed on a revolving stand close to the door, clearly uninterested.

Manuel turned to him; eyebrows pulled together in a deep V.

"¿Mande? She's my cousin too!" Protested Antonio, shrugging and letting go of the end of a scarf. He winked at me, a huge smile splitting his face.

"Well, yes, but only I can call her *Prima* like this," insisted Manuel, crossing his arms over his chest.

Antonio made as if to answer, but I cut in before things turned into a full-on scene from a *telenovela*.

"VATOS! ¿Qué pasa?" Dudes. What's up.

Their eyes locked for a tense moment as they glared at one another.

"Well??" I asked, tapping my foot impatiently. I hated their displays of machismo, which, luckily, were infrequent.

Manuel came back to reality first. He cleared his throat. "Oh, we wanted to ask you to take *comida* with us. We have news about the ..." his eyes skimmed the shop, presumably to make sure no one else was here.

Sofia had left just before they came in, so we were alone. Otherwise, of course, I wouldn't have yelled at them. What kind of businesswoman did he take me for, anyway? I huffed at the thought.

He continued. "... goings-on lately, especially about Millicent." His voice betrayed his unease with that subject. The look on his face was that of someone equally eager to know something—and to never find out.

The air around us seemed to thicken. *Now* they had my attention.

"I have news. You only know what I told you. So, I'm the one with the news, not you, not *we,"* Antonio said, almost puffing his chest out like a bird defending its territory, or a small boy in the schoolyard offended by some other small boy trying to steal his thunder.

And these were grown men, one with an important job, and the other a business owner? Where was the hope for humanity?

Antonio's face rearranged itself into part smirk, part frown, part *I'm-not-sure-how-to-look-for-this-prank* kind of face. Then he said it.

"Yes, *comida*, but not until after I arrest you for not telling me you *knew* Manuel killed Millicent Jones."

He pulled himself to his full height and pretended to reach to his waist for handcuffs, while forcing on a serious face. He failed miserably. Started to laugh as loud as Manuel had last night. To me, right now, he sounded like a hyena, an ugly one.

Several things happened at once.

If looks could kill, Manuel would have died on the spot. The air crackled with anger. Mine. *Death by Carli* would be engraved on his tombstone.

The music, which had been filling the air with a soothing guitar melody stopped at that very instant. Manuel's voice rang loudly in the sudden silence. In his defense, the music had stopped just as the first word exploded out of him.

"WHAT!? *¿QUÉ?* I TOLD YOU NOT TO TELL HER I TOLD YOU!"

He glared so hard at Antonio, one had to wonder how his eyeballs didn't leave their sockets and fly across the room like projectiles.

Antonio froze, his eyes directed at the floor, mouth puckered, his face turning a shade lighter as he suppressed a laugh.

I said nothing, just stood there, arms crossed, the atmosphere growing heavier with every one of my heartbeats, my breath coming fast and hard. I glared back and forth between them, desperate to say *I'm not going to comida*, but held back.

Because, if I didn't go, I wouldn't find out what happened to Mil. I didn't even ask why he wasn't waiting to tell me until dinner tonight. We couldn't talk about this in front of his date.

After his outburst, Manuel directed his eyes to the floor, the muscles in his jaw twitching, his shoulders hunched. I ignored him. Knowing what Antonio could tell me about the mystery was more important than berating Manuel for betraying me. For now.

So, reigning in all my mixed emotions and thoughts, nostrils flaring with every inhale, chest tightening, I pretended it didn't bother me nearly as much as it did. I would deal with Manuel later.

How had I ever believed there might be a chance for us? No way. Not with this betrayal, said my pride, my shame, my whatever it was I was feeling.

But the truth was that Antonio was almost as close to us as we were to one another. He'd have found out in time, during one of our long dinners, when shots of tequila were drunk before *and* after the dinner wine. Well, them drinking all that.

Instead of shooing them out the door and locking it behind them, I glared, my face, no, my whole self, seeming as if I'd been thrown into a bath of scorching water. My skin felt flushed, and I steamed. And, no doubt, my face reflected the color of that having happened. In other words, lobster red.

"Okay, *chicos*. Let's go." I said, my voice revealing a mix of exhaustion and defeat. I sighed with my entire body while I shooed them toward the door, me going out last so I could lock it.

Antonio opened his mouth and looked like he was going to say something, his lips parting and then pressing together in hesitation, but I didn't allow it.

My voice hit the walls as I unleashed a "*VAMOS!*" loud enough to make them both understand the door was not only closed on the subject but sealed shut with cement.

Just as we walked out of the courtyard and onto the sidewalk, the early afternoon sun still high above, the man who ran an upscale restaurant where no humble taco would *ever* grace the menu said, "How about going to Hank's? It's Taco Tuesday."

I rolled my eyes, but Antonio quickly approved. They also served what I considered good food, like salads and grilled fish, so I agreed.

Once seated, and after the boys wolfed down first one, then a second, order of tacos like starving men, while I ate a nice small grilled salmon filet with a salad, Antonio began to tell us the story. Well, tell me, since he'd already told Manuel, apparently.

My eyes narrowed, and my gaze drilled into my friends as if I could read their very thoughts.

But before he could say much, I made them both promise to tell no one, in or outside the family, about my suspicions regarding Manuel.

"Don't talk. Just listen, and after, no more talk about it!" I said, pointing my index finger at them.

It took little to get their agreement. I kept my voice steely; my words clear when I told them that if anyone ever brought it up to me, I said I'd assume they'd told.

And to return the favor—because my mother had raised a polite girl who always returned favors—I'd tell their current girlfriends, future girlfriends, and future wives, my voice tinged with a playful malice, about the time they both stayed up in a tree while me, a girl, ran to get a snake hook, ran back to where a snake lay, just below the tree where they waited each on a different branch, like oversized ornaments. I'd grabbed the four-foot-long snake with the hook, ran fifty yards to release it before running back to the tree. I could almost see and hear their hearts sink as I recounted the incident. They'd been petrified. Just petrified. Babies!

Their voices wavered as they protested. You were a year older than us. We couldn't see it so well from up there, hidden by the grass, and didn't know how big it might be. You never minded snakes. And other such excuses. But, in the end—their faces showing a reluctant acceptance and regret about missing out on all the fun of recounting the story to others—they agreed to the deal.

Finally, Antonio told the story I'd come to hear.

Chapter 23

A ntonio leaned in, his voice taking on a somber tone.

"Late yesterday afternoon, Denise Bouchard—she said you two had been at the same party as her and Millicent Jones," he said, traveling a finger between Manuel and me "had what you could call a spectacular meltdown.

"She called me at the station," Antonio continued, his eyes narrowing slightly as if piecing together a puzzle. "We've met a couple of times at events around here. She said she had something important to tell me about Millicent Jones."

My pulse quickened, my curiosity piqued.

He'd invited her to the station when she said she wanted to speak to him without her husband, Bill, present, which, of course, had set off his cop radar.

In Antonio's cramped office, within earshot of the bustling bullpen where phones rang constantly, where the distant chatter of cops discussing cases could be heard along with the muffled struggles of people being arrested, Denise, nervously peeling away at the sleeve on an El Café cup, had spilled everything like a bunch of rocks thrown down a slide in a children's playground.

She'd told him that Bill resisted taking the medication prescribed to him for depression. He did so much better when he was on it that she'd slip it to him when he tried to do without. She knew he'd skipped even before his mood changed sometimes because she counted his pills every day.

The night of the party, she'd added a crushed tablet of the medication, Elavil, to a glass of red wine from the bar ... and set it beside his place card.

No one else had been around, and she never imagined that someone would have the audacity to take it when it was clearly meant for someone else. People often switched seats or tables at the Música Clásica Esencial events, but usually not when that place was obviously occupied, like with wine right in front of someone's name card.

I glanced at Manuel, who had the grace to look sheepish.

Just then, a group of expats greeted Antonio when they entered the restaurant and sat at the next table, briefly distracting us. With pleasantries exchanged, Antonio resumed speaking, though the restaurant had filled up since our arrival and the sound of clanging dishes and chatter somewhat drowned out Antonio's voice, forcing me to lean in.

Denise had told Antonio that she knew Bill would drink the wine as soon as he sat, despite the fact he shouldn't have alcohol because of the meds. But he always had one glass at parties, and she usually didn't say anything about it. One glass wouldn't kill him, she reasoned, and sometimes, she decided it helped, because it relaxed him, and he at least got some medicine in him when she put the Elavil in it.

As she stood near the bar with Bill, who was engrossed in conversation with someone, she saw Millicent arrive and search for her place card, saw her sit at the table next to where they would be sitting. She watched Manuel arrive and stop to greet Mil

Then, Denise said, she'd continued to watch, horrified, her heart pounding like a drum in her chest, from across the garden. Said it had seemed like a dream to her.

Manuel getting Bill's wine and handing it to Mil. She wondered how it would affect Mil; her mind racing, torn between action and inaction, dread tightened around her stomach.

She considered running over to stop Mil from drinking the wine, but decided against it.

Bill couldn't find out she was putting his anti-depressant in his wine, in his anything, for that matter. It would become an issue between them. And no one else should know either.

What would they think? She was a nurse, after all. Even though retired, her professional ethics still deserved consideration. The chance of one dose killing him when combined with alcohol, or anyone, existed, but was *so* remote that most doctors who prescribed it didn't even tell their patients. They'd say that drinking alcohol while taking this medication wasn't recommended, but wouldn't explain further.

She'd gradually increased the dose in his wine or food, starting with a quarter pill and closely monitoring his reaction each time. Eventually, she reached a full dose without noticing any adverse effects on him.

Whenever he drank wine, she always made sure he had only one glass. Monitored him always, she'd told Antonio.

The metaphorical cogs in my mind clicked into place, like a lock finally opening. I bolted up in my seat, fully alert.

That nagging feeling that had clawed at the back of my thoughts when Lisa had revealed that Denise struggled with getting Bill to take his medication finally made sense.

And then, Amanda, her eyebrows slightly furrowed, mentioning how Denise had been rude to the staff. Now I realized that on some level, not knowing what Manuel had done, she must have blamed the missing wine fiasco on them.

Antonio continued the story. The more he told it, the more Manuel seemed to retreat into himself. His eyes dimmed and fixed on the table's surface. He looked distinctly uneasy, and deep in thought.

Denise had hoped nothing would happen to Mil from just one dose of an anti-depressant; it was so unlikely. Yet, had Mil been one of those rare people who could die from one dose when combined with alcohol?

Then, she recalled how much wine Mil always drank, and almost reversed her decision to not intervene. And, too late, she watched Mil, fascinated, as she gulped most of the wine.

She'd spent the evening in a near-agony of indecision.

The next day?

Mil dead.

How could that be? From just *one* dose?

Her guilt. Complete confusion. Wondering what medications Mil might have been prescribed that caused an interaction with Bill's Elavil and the alcohol.

At eighty-two years old, she must have been taking a prescription or two. She'd wondered what to say. What not to say. Just wait. No, come forward. The anguish of it all.

By yesterday, Denise thought her head would explode if she didn't confess. It was questionable to her that Bill's meds in Mil's drink had anything to do with her death, but she couldn't be sure. She knew something wasn't right, and as a nurse, she wondered about any connection she might have missed.

Plus, she so wanted to tell someone, *needed* to tell someone, anyone, about what she'd done; it had weighed on her, and the image of Mil gulping down the wine with the medicine in it kept popping into her thoughts like a cork bobbing on water, all day and night.

Now, Antonio said, "I didn't arrest her ... still don't have the lab reports, but one pill? It's possible it killed our victim, but she'd have to have been on a drug that caused a reaction when taken with Elavil. And wine."

"Did you tell the medical examiner?" I asked.

His eyes met mine, narrowing, lips pursed, eyes up to his brows as if wondering if I believed him unable to do his job.

"Yes, of course." He answered, in the tone of voice he used with strangers.

He then looked at Manuel while shaking his head to show his disappointment in me for asking.

"I saw that!" I said.

"Chicos," said Manuel, "no fighting." He said it with no heart in it. I understood. Though he hadn't killed her on purpose, Millicent might have still died because of him.

A server came to remove our now-empty plates while the bustle of the busy restaurant continued all around us.

"From what I found out, one dose of Elavil given to someone who doesn't need it and who's drinking might make them woozy and unfocused, but it shouldn't kill them," said Antonio.

"Shouldn't or wouldn't?" I asked.

He hesitated, then continued. "Shouldn't, but in some rare instances, it could. Depends on other drugs in their system."

We all sat in silence for a moment; Manuel's eyes fixated on the tablecloth again. It was as if he hoped to find the answer to the world's problems—or at least his own—hidden in its fabric.

"On its own, I doubt it would kill her," said Antonio. "Otherwise, we'd have a slew of dead people all the time because many people drink alcohol even when on anti-depressants. That's my main reason for not arresting her. And for me even telling you about it all."

He and Manuel locked eyes.

My heart pounded against my rib cage. Manuel might still be in deep trouble, even if he hadn't meant her harm.

In the end, Denise agreed to stay in town, and to give Antonio Bill's and her passports. She cried. Then she managed to collect herself, went home to grab the documents, and dutifully handed them over to Antonio.

"Wow, Antonio. That's a crazy story ..." I said.

We were all silent for a few minutes, each trapped in our own world of thoughts.

Manuel's eyes were wide and haunted, his lips slightly parted as if to speak, but no words came out. His face betrayed the horrifying realization of his possible involvement in the death of a woman, certainly made more real now that he knew for certain that a drug had been put into the wine she drank.

Antonio's gaze darted back and forth without really seeing anything, most likely caught between this case and his desire to be done with this conversation before we all met again tonight for dinner with his girlfriend.

And me? Consumed with anxiety, my thoughts tangled around Manuel's situation, his possible connection to Mil's death.

The unspoken fear that gnawed at us all hung in the air, a dark cloud that wouldn't disperse. Because if it proved that the Elavil and the wine combination was what killed Millicent, Manuel would be linked to her death, even if his action had been unintentional ... and that carried the heavy weight of an arrest, a trial, and quite possibly a prison sentence.

CHAPTER 24

F inally, Antonio spoke again. "Yes, a *loco* story. But also ..."

"What!?" I felt jumpy, and it showed in my voice.

"Well, there's other drugs in her system, but the coroner didn't have a conclusive result on what, yet. It's at the lab waiting to be tested. They've been extra busy."

"When?" Asked Manuel, the cop in him coming out, or perhaps impatience over knowing whether he'd played a part in her death.

"No sé, vato ...," replied Antonio. He didn't know.

My mind hit gridlock. So many clues of the pharmacology variety piling up about Mil's death. So, Denise might, or might not, have killed Mil, even if not intentionally. And Manuel would be responsible, too, even though unintentional.

But what were the other drugs in her system?

"Antonio, how many drugs does that make in her body, did you say?"

His eyes drilled into mine in mean cop mode. He always acted offended when I asked him specific questions about cases, but he always ended up telling me. Why not skip the dramatics? Nope.

Our Antonio was Mexican through and through. If there was a drama to be enacted, a moment where he could act more macho than he really was, you could count on him to perform.

"Seems like three now. No thinking. We can only make stuff up until we get news back. Let's order dessert."

"Yeah, forget dead people, no dessert on earth is safe from you, we all know that," retorted Manuel, grinning.

The remark didn't stop our Antonio from waving down the server.

A cup of coffee—no matcha at Hank's, which I didn't understand—and a sugar free cheesecake later, I headed back to work after we all agreed to see one another at dinner. I thought of stopping at El Café, just a few doors down from Hank's, for matcha, but I'd already had three cups.

I found the shop buzzing with customers, Esme doing her best to keep up. A couple of men were debating over a leather couch, eventually deciding to measure the space for it at home before buying it. They asked me to hold it 'til the end of the day.

A woman wanted to haggle over a dark-colored Celine dress with a ruffled skirt that didn't suit her. I gave Esme *the look*, the one that said *this woman can't walk out of my shop with that dress*, so, as pre-planned for such situations, Esme sauntered over to me and the customer.

We guided her towards another Celine dress, shorter and in lavender, which complemented her much better. She finally agreed. I took immense pride in helping women find the right outfit.

In the late afternoon, I pondered what to wear to dinner, having tried to put any thoughts of the mayhem in town out of my mind. I needed to distance myself from it. Ideas about who else, what else, might have done in Mil would come after I gave myself a break from thinking about it, I reasoned.

I wanted to impress Antonio's new girlfriend. He'd told her about my business, of course he had. It made me proud, but also self-conscious about others' opinions until they saw how I dressed, or they visited the store.

Many of my regulars said they only shopped resale with me and nowhere else. I grinned, deciding to wear a stunning short Valentino caddy dress, beige Gianvitto Rossi ankle boots, and a Bottega Veneta bag. Sophisticated and perfect for any city. *She'll assume I went to Neiman Marcus in Dallas to dress for this dinner*. And then she'd discover it all came from here. Things might, or might not, work between her and Antonio, but she'd show up at my shop for sure. I smiled, visualizing her crossing my threshold.

My phone buzzed. I snatched it from my pocket, smiling when I saw a text from Antonio.

can you talk for a minute?

Instead of texting back, I called him.

"Did she ditch you already, and you're calling to cancel dinner?" I asked, grinning.

"Nope, well ..." I heard a tired smile in Antonio's voice.

"*¿Qué pasa*, Antonio?" His exhausted but intense vibe caused the hairs on the back of my neck to stand at attention, as if bracing me for an attack.

"I am canceling dinner, but not because of her."

"What, then?" I asked, surprised.

"I can't say. It's work." He spoke abruptly.

"Oh?"

"Well, you'll find out soon enough. But I really, really, can't tell you right now, Carli. Okay? Don't ask me again. How about we meet up tomorrow, and then I'll tell you?"

"Well, okay, I guess. Does Manuel know?"

"No, Carli, tried calling, but he didn't answer."

"Okay, well, breakfast? What time?"

"Not sure yet, *Prima*, okay? I'll text. I got to go. Bye!" He hung up.

I gazed at the phone in my hand, not knowing what to think. He sure seemed tense. Well, so much for showing off my Valentino. I shrugged.

CHAPTER 25

A ntonio called me first thing the next morning before I'd even left my bed. Groggy, I grabbed the phone from my nightstand and answered.

"Hola, Antonio. You coming over now?" I asked, eager to find out what was happening.

"No, I can't, Carli. So sorry." He said.

I sat straight up on the bed and Dap joined me as if he could understand the conversation, too.

"But you promised!" I exclaimed.

"I know. Wait! I said I can't *meet*; I didn't say I would not tell you what happened."

"So. Tell me." Was the man dense?

Chaotic energy sparked between us along the phone line. It was just how we were, sometimes clashing in our own special way, a crazy dance that was pretty much the norm for us.

"Well. A neighbor of Mil's was found dead in her house yesterday."

My eyes bugged out as inhaled air like a dying commodity, while he let out a quick, frustrated sigh.

"A friend found her. About an hour before I called you to cancel dinner. I... I think you might know her."

"WHO?" I shouted.

He hesitated. "*Prima*, you can't tell anybody yet, okay?"

When I didn't respond, because, frankly, my mouth wouldn't work, he asked again. "You won't tell?"

It burst out of me like lava from a volcano.

"No, Antonio! WHO?"

His breath reached me in spurts, like that of a long-distance runner at the end of a race.

"Okay, don't shoot the messenger. Babette Miller." He said her name all in a rush, as if it would run away from him if he spoke slower.

"WHAT?" *What was going on?*

As if by agreement, silence filled the line for a moment.

Babette Miller? Why?

"But, but I don't understand. Why Babette too?

"OH, MY GOD, ANTONIO!"

Now his turn to yell.

"WHAT?" He caught himself and lowered his voice and asked again, "What, Carli?" Weariness laced his words.

Should I tell him? Was it relevant? Would telling him help, or hurt, my own investigation? Which, of course, could not end now, not with this new development.

I wanted to win, to find out who'd done it. I needed to discuss it with my dead father. Yes. Quick discussion in my head. No time for the usual ritual with the photo.

But ... Antonio *was* the cop here, not me ...

What to do?

Was it time to share what I'd found at Janice's? And the memory it brought back to me which matched it and, in a way, confirmed its validity?

"Carli?" He asked again, tension wrapped like barbed wire around my name.

I took a deep breath and plunged in. "Antonio, I saw Babette at Mil's house yesterday."

Silence. Silence, that is, except for my heart slamming up against my rib cage.

"Really? When?" He asked calmly, back in professional cop mode.

I had walked to the kitchen during our exchange, surprised to find myself standing at the window, as if transported there.

Dap jumped on the kitchen counter, using one of the stools next to where I stood. I jumped nearly as high as he had.

"Dap! You scared me!"

He responded by sitting straight up like a perfect gentleman right in front of me, fixed his eyes on mine, blinked, then meowed plaintively. I imagined him frustrated to have no words to say what he wanted to tell me.

Distracted by him, I didn't hear what Antonio said.

"What, Antonio?"

"There, see, when you talk to cats, you miss what humans are saying."

"Okay, okay, but, what?"

"I said, we think it might be related to Mil's death, so you seeing her at Mil's house is interesting."

I could almost see him thinking, imagining his furrowed brow, his pinched lips.

"At first glance, it seems she might have ingested drugs of some sort. Also, it probably has nothing to do with it, but when the friend who found her arrived, Puccini's Tosca was playing on her CD player on a loop. It's just that, well, Mil had been at that Música Clásica Esencial opera and party, and Tosca *is* about murder, after all."

He paused for a second, then asked, "What were you doing over there?" Said the cop.

"Realmente, Antonio? I didn't kill the woman. I said I *saw* her. We didn't even talk while she was at Mil's."

"Carli, can we stop with the jousting? Two women are dead."

"You started it!" I caught myself acting like a child. Changed my tone.

Because, really, it was my guilt about breaking into Janice's house and the fact I hadn't told him about it yet. My insides twisted at the thought of telling him I'd gone into her home without her permission.

"Babette called me in late morning and asked if the dress we were altering for her was ready yet. She just got back into town and she ... oh no." Tears came to my eyes.

"What?" Asked Antonio.

I sighed.

"She was going to wear it to a dinner party tonight," I mumbled.

"Oh. Sorry you lost your friend, Carli." My friend and cousin was back.

"She wasn't a friend, not really, but a good customer, and I knew her well enough, I suppose." I sniffed.

"So, what happened when you saw her?"

"She'd asked if I could have the dress delivered to her house, she'd pay extra. I was having Esme dusting all the handbag and shoe shelves, so I decided to take the dress to her myself."

"So ... if you were going there, how did you end up seeing her at Mil's?"

"The taxi came really fast, and traffic moved fast, too. So, I got there fifteen minutes early, and had the cab drop me off at the end of the street to get a bit of fresh air. It's when I was about four houses away from hers that I noticed her farther down the street, opening the courtyard door to Mil's. I called out, but she was already inside, and didn't hear me."

I stopped. Took a deep breath. Tried to stop the tears that threatened.

"And?" Asked Antonio. I sensed pretend patience in the one word.

"Well, so, I went into the courtyard, but the front door was already closed behind her. I knocked once or twice, but no one came, so, curious, I went to the back of the house. She was sitting at the kitchen table with Liam, and it looked like they were about to share a meal."

I stopped and recalled Babette's smile, her relaxed demeanor. Smiling and relaxed. The thought had come to me that no one had told her about Mil yet. Liam had had his back to me, so no idea how he might have looked.

"Go on," said Antonio.

"Well, not sure why, but I decided to not say anything and to go wait for Babette in her courtyard. She's one of those who doesn't lock her street door during the day."

"I wish people would do that. Those doors are there for a reason, for protection," said the cop.

"Anyway, she showed up about ten minutes later. I didn't mention that I followed her to Mil's and left because it seemed silly."

Dap reminded me of his presence with a loud meow, and by rubbing his face against my hand.

"Carli, it's not your fault. Babette's body is on its way to Queré-taro already. Best if the same coroner works on her, too."

"She seemed different by the time she arrived home. I realized Liam had told her. About Mil, I mean. She was crying.

"She looked at me, and me at her, and we hugged. You know. I just cannot, cannot, believe this is happening in our town."

My own eyes had been moist by then, and they were damp now.

He remained silent, probably thinking about all the crimes I blissfully ignored. My self-imposed ignorance kept my bubble nice and cozy, but the recent happenings had shattered that illusion. The mystery gnawed at me, and I had to unravel it, had to dig into what was happening in my town, within my own circle. This grated on Antonio.

He'd been angry with me when he'd found out about what I'd done in New York. He feared for my safety, of course, but he also didn't like me getting involved in what he considered "dangerous work." In his opinion, women shouldn't engage in that. This attitude just made me roll my eyes.

But, really, other than getting involved when people I knew died, yes, I lived in a happy bubble. By choice.

Why dwell on the cartels that had invaded even my beautiful hometown, warring, extorting, and killing? I'd turned my back on that darkness, choosing instead to embrace Mexico's beauty, the warmth of its people, and the joy of living in such a sun-kissed place.

"Carli. Stuff like this happens all over the world all the time. Not just here. You *know* that. We'll get to the bottom of it, and things will settle down after that. Again, I'm sorry you lost two customers to this."

"Oh, Antonio, I don't care about losing customers in this way! What do you take me for? These were breathing, living women!" I started to cry.

"Aw, Carli, don't cry, *princesa. Por favor.*"

"Why? Because your machismo can't take it?" I retorted, lashing out at him for things he had no control over.

"Okay, I have to go. Don't do anything stupid. Stay out of it. I *know* you! *Ciao.*"

"I'm sorr ..." I wanted to apologize for my meanness to him when he was trying to be kind, but he'd already hung up. He had two murders to solve and didn't need a snarky, sniveling female on his hands.

So, now, Babette was dead too, from apparent poisoning. Or was it an overdose?

Babette Miller. Not a close friend, but a regular buyer and seller at my shop, someone I'd wave to around town, had coffee with on occasion, Mil's neighbor from four doors down, a writer, member of Música Clásica Esencial. Same circle.

Did it go back to the music? I couldn't help but wonder.

But that made no sense. Who would want to kill members of a classical music non-profit, one that supported world-class musicians by bringing their superb music to our mid-sized mountain town, and ran an education outreach program for music students?

And sure, both women visited my shop on a regular basis, but why kill my customers? Women who only sought to look good? I ignored the quickening of my heartbeat, turning from the thought. Of course, only a coincidence.

Babette and Mil socialized together often. If forced to choose, I'd have named Babette as Mil's best friend in town. What might the connection be?

Best friends, Música Clásica Esencial members, writers, Babette more so than Mil, customers at Carli's Secret Closet. A headache formed at my temples like a gathering of dark clouds, so I stopped the mental gymnastics.

Another link between them came to mind. They both knew Janice. And the way our call had ended, I hadn't told Antonio about my discovery at Janice's house and about the conversation I'd overheard all those months ago at Café Monet.

I walked to the kitchen. Put my hand on the kettle. I stared out the window into my neighbor's garden, at the bird of paradise plant growing to the right of the sliding glass door into the house. It had flowered since the last time I'd seen it. How had they gotten it to do that? Flower so fast? I'd looked at it yesterd ... *what* was I doing, wondering about the flowers in the Gonzalezes' yard?

Another woman dead and I'm worried about *that*?

The phone rang. The display lit up with Manuel's name and picture. I'd taken it at Sunday *comida*, out by the oak tree that stood, tall, wide, and beautiful, about halfway between our parents' houses.

You couldn't see it in the small photo, but he'd been leaning on it and had just stopped laughing out loud at me for spilling champagne on my blouse after telling him over and over—despite his warnings to the contrary—that I could carry the flute and take a photo, all while walking on the rocky ground in heels. When I'd snapped the photo, his eyes had still twinkled with the remnants of his laughter.

I shook my head, fanning my hands quickly back and forth in front of my chest, desperate to erase the dreadful sensation lodged in my heart. But that nagging unease growing inside me didn't go away. I sensed a sourpuss look forming on my face, but it seemed as though it belonged to someone else.

The phone stopped ringing. And started right back up again.

"Hola, Manuel," said a woman in a small voice. Me.

"Carlitaaaa?"

"Sí?"

"You okay?"

"Sí."

"Where you at?"

"I'm fine." *Fine* came out harsher than I'd intended.

"Where are you, *Prima?*" Now he sounded annoyed.

"Home. I just talked to Antonio and he ..."

"He told me."

A deep sigh traveled all the way from his end of the phone line to mine.

"What's happening, Manuel?"

"I'm coming over to you. *Esperamé.*"

"No. I can't wait. I have to go to work."

Actually, no way was I going to work right now.

"Don't go *anywhere.* I'll be right over. Don't go do anything stupid!"

I heard myself tell him goodbye in my smallest voice. I put the phone down on the counter as if it were the most delicate and precious thing I owned.

Chapter 26

M anuel showed up at my doorstep within the hour, wearing that infectious smile of his despite the trouble he faced.

He followed me up to the rooftop deck, where the city's skyline stretched out like a beautiful painting. There, we shared a carafe of French pressed coffee. I kept a stash of Jamaican Blue Mountain coffee for him in my freezer. Couldn't serve my favorite chef any old brew, after all. And with him, I sometimes had coffee instead of matcha.

We each poured ourselves a cup, the rich aroma filling the air with hints of caramel, the smell being my favorite part of coffee.

Our conversation calmed me. Manuel wanted to be sure I didn't involve myself in anything else that might harm me. I should never have gone to Janice's house without her permission.

We talked about how to let Antonio know about the letter at her house without implicating me. Manuel thought I should go see him and just say it. No way. Guilt flooded through me whenever I remembered that Manuel wasn't aware that I had the letter in my possession.

For several minutes, we weren't able to talk because the bells at the Parroquia tolled, a wedding by the sound of it, since after only a few minutes, the sounds of a *Callejoneada*—the traditional parade that took place right after a wedding party left the church—reached us.

In the parade, the groom, bride, and their guests followed two people wearing large puppet costumes, known as *Mojigangas*, dressed in wedding clothes, who turned in circles while leading the procession. A *Banda de Viento*, a mariachi band, followed behind, and somewhere in there would be a donkey carrying tequila with servers pouring it into the cups that wedding guests had been given to hang from their necks with an attached string. All would be smiling large and loving life by the time they got to the location of the reception.

Death and joy melded together in one moment. How could it be?

And why did Antonio and Manuel always think I'd do something "stupid"? Just because I wanted to solve a little ol' murder? It didn't mean I did stupid stuff, *sí*? If they weren't happy about that, they should solve the danged thing themselves. I huffed at the thought, and Dap, who had been following me non-stop around the house since yesterday—as if spying for those two, I couldn't help thinking—meowed.

Manuel offered to cook us breakfast, and we headed downstairs to my kitchen.

He cooked us up some *huevos rancheros*—he made the best I'd ever had—adding a secret spice he wouldn't even tell *me* about.

Eventually, he seemed to think he'd calmed me down enough, so he left.

At odds, knowing I must tell Antonio about Janice, I decided to send him an email about it. If I texted, he'd call me right away and might even come over here or go to the shop to find me. That meant I couldn't be at either location until he'd had some time to calm down after reading my email.

My heart thumped away like the rabbit in that story, Thumper, the one who thumped his left hindfoot when he was anxious.

So, where would Antonio not think of looking?

I could go to Liam's and sort through Mil's clothes! Plus, he might know something about Babette since she'd been at his house the day before. My suspicions about him had waned considerably due to Janice and the letter.

Still, unease lingered inside me. The kind that comes when we tell ourselves something is a sure thing, but our feelings tell us otherwise. Like that.

Then, I realized that if Janice had killed Mil, it didn't explain Babette's murder. I mean, she had nothing to do with what I had on Janice. At least, I didn't think so.

But even if Liam had killed his mother, why would he kill Babette, too? That made no sense either. A successful Dallas developer wasn't going around San Miguel killing older classical music lovers. Babette must just be a coincidence. I didn't really believe in them, but that didn't mean they never happened.

If I put paranoia aside, Liam was innocent. And that letter incriminated Janice, at least as far as Mil went.

Confusion reigned in my mind.

Nevertheless, something made me call Liam and say I had a sudden opening in my schedule. I could go to his house to look at Mil's clothes. And in the process, hide for a while from Antonio and Manuel who would both be so angry. Antonio, because I had gone into Janice's house without her permission and not only read, but taken, a letter relevant to a murder investigation. And Manuel, because I allowed him to assume that I'd only looked at the letter, not taken it with me.

In the end, Liam and I agreed on eleven-thirty, which gave me an hour to get there.

I called Sofia at the shop and said not to expect me until after *comida*. Followed that with a text to Esme to alert her that I'd be in, but later in the afternoon.

I got my laptop and wrote an email to Antonio. I decided against copying Manuel on it. For this sort of thing, and because I was involved, I believed that Antonio would tell Manuel.

I wanted them both calm when I next saw them, that's all. And an afternoon away should be long enough for them to forgive me, or start to forgive me, for not telling anyone about this sooner.

Dear Antonio,

I need to say something I'm scared to tell you in person because of how you'll react.

You really need this, though, so I can't hide it anymore.

You see, I went to Janice Johnson's house and found something. Janice is a friend of Mil's, or was.

Yes, I went while she wasn't at home, and without her permission because I was suspicious of her, and I worried about Manuel being accused (as you now know). I used the key she gave me so I could send my maid to water her plants when she's out of town. There, it's out.

Please try to realize that this goes a long way for you to solve the murder. At least Mil's. I've been afraid to tell you because I knew you'd be angry. You and Manuel.

I found a letter in a desk drawer at Janice's. The letter says that if Mil dies, Janice's debt to her is excused. At the very same moment I read the letter, something came to my mind, a conversation I heard at Café Monet many months ago, maybe even a year.

I'd been there waiting for Luna to come have comida with me. Mil arrived soon after me and sat at the next table; she was with Mercedes Barrera, you know, the lawyer.

As you know, Mil wasn't a quiet talker. Soon after they sat, I heard her tell Mercedes that after she was gone, she didn't see the point of her estate going after those to whom she'd made personal loans, that it wasn't much, considering her net worth, but that the estate should pursue any business loans she'd made.

Mercedes retorted that Mil's son might object, but Mil just chuckled at that. I didn't hear anything after because Luna arrived. And you know how she makes an entrance!

She was wearing a sleek looking royal blue pantsuit with cigarette pants. She'd gotten it from my shop, of course. The pants ended at the ankle so she could show off her up-to-there-heels, yellow Louboutin toeless platform pumps with studs. Wow, right?

Anyway, you didn't need to know that about Luna. But, as you can see, I wanted to tell you about Janice because she must be guilty, at least of killing Mil.

Please forgive me for not telling you sooner, and for taking the letter with me (I didn't mean to do that, I swear! I'll tell you how that happened later).

Abrazos y mucho amor,

Carli

CHAPTER 27

As soon as I clicked Send on my email to Antonio, I set out for Mil's house, my tablet, and phone in my tote bag (Givenchy), ready to take photos of Mil's clothes, excited about what treasures I'd find there.

Then, guilt came over me. How dare I be happy about that when the only reason I was getting those clothes was because she had died? I reminded myself that whether anyone triaged her clothes or not, she'd still be gone. And I continued to walk toward her house in the *Colonia* San Antonio.

After fifteen minutes of walking at a brisk pace, or rather, as at quick a pace as cobblestoned sidewalks allowed, I arrived at the house.

I rang the bell at the street door and waited, looking toward Babette's house. Sadness for both women whose lives had been taken too soon dazed me—their age didn't matter, an abrupt end such as theirs hadn't been in their plans.

The door opened to Liam. He looked worse than the last time I'd seen him. More lines seemed to mar his face, dark half-moons filled the space under his eyes, and his hair need-ed shampooing. His shirt looked like it had been slept in. He seemed even thinner, too. Or was I imagining that? I suppose that if my *mamá* died abruptly, I'd drop some pounds, too. Who wanted to eat under such circumstances?

His mother—and her best friend—dead under suspicious cir-cumstances.

I hesitated, but then followed him through the courtyard and to the front door. When we entered the house, its gloominess overcame me, a dark cloak thrown over a sad situation, a dark cloud lingering after a storm.

Behind that, though, I sensed something else, something dif-ficult to define. Was I making something out of nothing, or did a real concern exist? Would I regret my decision to hide from Antonio and Manuel by coming here?

Perhaps it hadn't been such a good idea, but I brushed it aside.

Besides, I might find out something that would help me solve the murders.

"Want some coffee, Carli?" Liam asked as soon as he opened the door to the house, though his tone of voice told me he didn't want to make coffee. He said it automatically, like muscle memory, not hospitality.

"No, thank you, had my quota today," I said, smiling.

Watching myself put one foot in front of the other, I ventured into the foyer. I stood there, unsure how to proceed. My heart and mind were at odds: Go. Don't go. Why was I so conflicted?

He nodded at my answer for the longest time, his face twitch-ing, arms crossed, staring at me with bloodshot eyes. His gaze flicked around the room like he'd forgotten where he was. When had the man last slept?

"You look unwell, Liam, if you don't mind me saying. I know this is a tough time for you, but I hope you're taking care of yourself. You deserve care, no matter what's happened with ... your mom." I said as gently as possible. Gulped when he didn't answer, wondering if I'd overstepped.

Tears formed in his eyes. With something lingering in the back of them, something . . . ominous? No. My imagination, surely. I needed to stop this speculation and get on with the reason I'd come here.

Still, he said nothing.

"So ... the clothes?" I asked into the awkward silence.

"Oh, yes, of course. My bad."

He'd forgotten why I'd come?

"It's okay, Liam. You have a lot on your mind."

I smiled again, giving him the benefit of the doubt, though it seemed to be unraveling . . .

From nowhere—and everywhere at once—a loud buzzer sounded.

Before my psyche could figure out it had come from the kitchen—one of those aggressive kitchen timers—my body jerked and I nearly shrieked.

The kitchen timer realization hit me as the scream started, so instead of full-blown, it came out like Dap when strangled, or rather, how he'd sound *if* strangled. Of course, I'd never strangle my Dapperoo!

Liam jolted at my reaction. We stood there for a few seconds, eyes locked, each trying to figure out the other's paranoia.

He spoke first. "Just . . . hmm . . . I put a chicken pot pie in the oven?" He said it as though asking me, his eyes crazed. Like he couldn't remember if that was the truth or a story he was making up.

That's when I smelled the pot pie. Realized the ordinariness of it and relaxed. Well, relatively, anyway. At least, my breathing returned to a rhythm nearer to normal.

Liam gazed at me, and I wondered if he didn't look a little like a lion appraising possible prey.

That thought bounced off the walls of my skull like a scream in a canyon. I saw Liam talking, but couldn't make out his words. My angst was so high now that my ears rang.

"What was that?" I asked, pulling myself together.

Liam frowned at me, eyes squinting, and zeroed in on mine.

"I said," he repeated, in the tone of voice one might use when speaking to a young child who only understands if spoken to really, really, slow . . . , "are you ready to go up to my mom's bedroom?"

The look on his face said he wondered about my state of mind, but there was definitely something else behind it, a nervousness, uncertainty. He rubbed the back of his neck and shifted his weight, like the question cost him something.

I shrugged off whatever was happening in that mind of mine and focused on him.

"Ah, yes. Yes, of course." I cleared my throat.

"Are you alright?" He asked, his head tilted, frown lines tight.

"Yes, sorry. I just realized I might have left a pot simmering on my stove."

It fit, right? Him talking about cooking reminding me of my own kitchen? I could use that as an excuse to leave, though wasn't it ridiculous? Deep breaths, I told myself.

The kitchen buzzer went off again, startling both of us this time.

"I better get that," he said, and headed for the kitchen.

As he walked, looking over his shoulder at me, he asked, "Do you need to go back?"

Did he mean go take the fictitious pot off my stove?

No. I needed to focus and not allow my most-likely misguided feelings, unwarranted fear, to get the best of me.

My mind wanted to stay put. My body? It wanted to turn around and leave *pronto*.

Yet . . . a compulsion to stay overwhelmed me, a tsunami overcoming a beach. I didn't understand it but decided to follow it. Plus, I needed to hide from Antonio, and even from Manuel, for a few hours.

I heard Liam mess around in the kitchen. Drawers opening and closing. The sound of something metal. And had a crazy thought.

What if he were looking for a knife to bring upstairs with him?

CHAPTER 28

I shook the thought away, but another one butted up right on its tail, as if following the Pied Piper.

What if he killed me? Here? Upstairs?

What? Why would he do that?

Liam came back into the foyer and asked. "There's enough potpie for two. It's one of those from City Market. You know, the large ones. You want some? Maybe after we go through the clothes?"

"Oh, well, I might. After, yes." I said, to humor him, but something in his eyes gave me pause.

He stood in front of me, face drawn, arms crossed, scratching at the crook of his elbows, face twitching. Had he slept at all since he'd arrived in San Miguel?

"Well, okay, let's go on up, then," he said, waving his arm as an invitation for me to go up ahead of him.

He seemed to sense my hesitation and added, "Sure you don't want to go home first to take that pot off the stove?"

I forced a smile, brushing off my concerns. See? He'd let me leave if that's what I wanted. Bloodshot eyes from a lack of sleep and an unkempt appearance from stressing and grieving over the sudden death of a loved one did not mean one was a killer, after all. And besides, Janice must have done it. She had the most powerful motivation. Liam already had plenty of his own money from what I knew.

"No, I'm fine, Liam, *gracias*. I don't think I left that pot on the stove after all. I'll follow you."

"No, no, go ahead." He waved me up the staircase.

So, I put my right foot on the first step, my left on the second, and so on.

On the way up, though, my mind flipped back to suspecting Liam.

But then I was caught up in the beauty of the wrought-iron balustrade, a temporary escape from my growing unease. At the top, I waited for him to point the way to Mil's bedroom, which I'd never entered.

He directed me to the second door on the right, the one farthest from the staircase.

I entered the bedroom, and my mouth dropped open at what I saw. An entire wall—at least twenty feet long—was nothing but sliding closet doors, all open.

Miles of clothing hung in them, a kaleidoscope of colors greeting me. About half the length consisted of double rods, and the other half single rods. Impressive. I'd never seen so many clothes in one person's home. My shop held more, of course, but you'd expect that.

The businesswoman in me speculated on how much such a loot would bring my shop in profit, but also how long it would take to sell them all. Of course, not all of them would fit the high standards of Carli's Secret Closet. Still, I'd never seen Mil in anything but high-quality clothing, even when running into her at the Saturday Organic Market, a casual environment.

"Why did she need so many clothes?" Asked Liam, in rhetorical fashion.

I shrugged in answer, a small smile escaping me. A man wouldn't understand.

"Well, what do you think?" He asked, still looking at the closet.

I turned to him, a light comment about Mil's fashion sense on the tip of my tongue, but the words died in my throat seeing how forlorn he looked. Instead, I addressed my task here.

"Liam, I won't be able to go through all this today. There's so much ..."

The closets were full to bursting with clothes, like overfilled Santa bags with toys falling out.

"Yes. I see that."

His voice brimmed with emotion, and I turned toward him again. His eyes glistened as he gazed at the clothes.

"I'm so sorry, Liam. This must be difficult for you."

He said nothing, and instead stood, his arms still crossed, mouth turned down, eyes in the same squint I'd noticed earlier. A wave of empathy rose in me. Except, my unease crept up again, nearly replacing it. He sank into the settee at the foot of the queen-sized bed set against the wall opposite the closets, his posture defeated, shoulders slumped. His eyes darted around the room, but avoided mine.

Him sitting down gave me a clear way, and perhaps time enough to get out the bedroom door should I decide to follow my getting-stronger-by-the-minute instinct to leave.

I turned away from him and faced the closet wall instead, realizing that Mil had been found in this very room, in this bed. I had to look away from it. Out of respect. Or fear. Or dismay. Or all three.

I took out my tablet, and on impulse, before opening the file into which I'd jot down details about the clothes, finger shaking, I engaged the recording app on it.

I decided to not question my action, to just do it, as the Nike slogan always encouraged us all to do.

At that moment, I realized that music played faintly in the room.

"What's that?" I asked.

Liam looked up at me, his face blank.

"The music. I hear something."

"Oh, that. Mom always kept this running in here. Especially when she slept."

He pointed to an Amazon Echo on a dresser, a surprising find considering Mil's age.

"A couple of years back, she wanted quiet music playing while she slept, but couldn't find a CD player that could play on repeat," Liam explained. "So that Christmas, I brought her the Alexa. Showed her how to ask for the music she wanted and how to time it so it would last through the night."

"She must have loved that." I whispered.

"Yes. From then on, I noticed that it always played whenever I was in her room. So, well, I've kept it playing the whole time since I've been here, too. Just changed it from classical to ..." He trailed off, nodding his head toward Alexa, now playing a new age vibe.

Was he sleeping in here? I wondered, surprised. A quick glance around pointed to a no. Only women's items in sight.

It also became obvious that the room had recently been thoroughly cleaned, most likely after the police left and Mil's body had been removed.

Suddenly, Liam grabbed a decorative pillow from the settee, fingers digging into it, and hugged it tight against his chest. His face crunched up, a painful scowl, and the corners of his mouth turned down so much he looked like a sad clown in a circus. He began to pick at loose threads on the embroidery of the pillow, a restless energy at work. A deep, jagged breath passed through him. He roughly wiped his eyes with the back of his hand, leaving visible tear streaks on his cheeks. His voice broke when he tried to speak, conveying a depth of pain no words could capture.

Then, as if he couldn't hold it back any longer, Liam's expression hardened. The soft sorrow in his eyes transformed into a cold, impenetrable stare. I watched his jaw tense, his lips pressing together in a thin line, his brow furrow. I realized with shock that it was anger bubbling up inside him. A quiet, simmering rage that was somehow more chilling than any outburst he might have had.

Spellbound, I didn't know what to say. What to do. What does one say to a man who looks so tortured?

Any warmth that had lingered on his face was replaced by an icy mask, both foreign and frightening. A chill ran down my spine, my heart pounding with fear.

What was I looking at in those eyes?

I searched his face for a reassuring sign, but found none.

A tightening sensation in my chest made it hard to breathe. Could I convince myself that it was nothing but unwarranted fear?

Something told me that this time it might be different. That it was different.

Why had I not listened to my intuition earlier when Liam gave me the chance to go back home to my fictitious pot on the stove?

Heart on overdrive like a runaway train, I fumbled to pull my phone from the front pocket of my favorite skinny jeans, fingers shaking.

I checked if any emails or texts had come in. Nothing. Had Antonio not read my email yet? Would he reply once he did? Should I try to text him? Or Manuel? Or Luna, Amy, anyone? They'd reply and become concerned if I didn't respond. Best not.

Once again, following another compulsion, I engaged the recording app on my phone. In case the one on the tablet gave out or missed some part of our conversation. Then, I went ahead as if all was well, and perhaps it was.

Just a grieving son.

We all did strange things when under stress.

"Well, Liam, I'll get started, okay?"

Tablet in hand, phone back in my pocket, I turned toward the closets again to decide where to start, willing the eyes in the back of my head to keep an eye on him.

"I'll start at the far end with the double rods. I don't think I'll get much farther than that today."

"If only she'd *helped* me," Liam whined.

I froze. What?

"I asked, you know." He seemed lost now and spoke as if he were alone in the room.

The hairs on the back of my neck stood at attention, small soldiers prepping for war. A shiver traveled from the bottom of my spine to the top of my head at the speed of a shuttle leaving Earth for the space station.

I pirouetted toward him like a ballerina on tiptoes, as if on a self-propelled swivel, rather than turning of my own volition.

I opened my mouth to ask what he meant, but closed it again, as if closing a child's bedroom door slowly and quietly when the child had just fallen asleep, not daring to breathe so as not to wake him or her.

"They're vultures. Vultures, I tell you."

His voice rose to a shout, his face a perfect description of anger and frustration, and turning a deep red. His eyes, wild and unseeing, pierced through the room. He shook his head back and forth, fists clenched at his sides, consumed by the emotion of the moment.

Did he still see me standing right here in front of him? Would he come out of the trance he'd clearly entered if I tiptoed out?

But then, I'd ... Liam cut off my thoughts and stopped my heart with what he said next.

"I just needed one hundred thousand. That's it! That's all!"

Liam's voice cracked, the desperation in his tone palpable. I saw his hands trembling uncontrollably. Saw the frantic, wild look in his eyes, his pain, his need, almost palpable. "To hold them off a while."

My heart froze mid-heartbeat.

I stood, rooted to the spot, trying to comprehend the magnitude of his confession.

One hundred thousand? Did I want to know what that meant?

The room blurred as my mind whirled with my new realization of who Liam most likely really was.

The truth of what I now believed he'd most likely done.

The moment would haunt me. Would define everything that came next.

Chapter 29

"Liam? What ... what are you saying?"

"You know." He whispered, eyes downcast.

"No, I don't ... I'm not sure."

I kept my eyes glued to the floor—because if I looked at him, he might come out of his reverie. I made myself as invisible as possible, as unremarkable as a street statue one passes by every day.

He rocked slightly, back and forth, his fingers pulling at invisible threads on his pants.

"And then. Urgh! That dealer coming back into my LIFE ..." He whined, grabbing his hair with both hands, face contorted in defeat as he leaned over the pillow.

Here was someone who seemed to have given up a fight against the devil. A man with possibly no hope left. But was that real despair—or manipulation? Or both?

No. No, I didn't want to believe that. Any second now, he'd tell me something else to take away what he seemed to be saying.

Instead, he said this.

"It's the danged drugs, Carli. Danged drugs!" He wailed.

I stifled a scream when he said my name. He *did* realize I still stood here, not five feet away from him!

Discretely, instinctively, prey doing its best to evade a predator in broad daylight, my heart pounding, I slid my left foot an inch or two toward the door, as if I were making myself more comfortable, as if such a small step might get me any closer to freedom.

The ridiculousness of me coming here alone hit me. What an *idiota* I'd been.

Ignoring my instincts about Liam had been a mistake. Why had I not listened to Manuel and Antonio warning me to stay out of things? But my compulsion to *know* had overridden everything. My bio-father's voice in my head told me to keep cool, to find a way out. *Well, how?*

The volume of the music rose on its own just then, as if to give more emphasis to the goings-on. A Sarah Brightman piece when Nirvana was called for, considering the energy in the room now.

I should have told Manuel I'd be coming here. Antonio. Esme. Luna. Someone. Anyone.

Like a jack-in-the-box, Liam jumped from the settee and rushed to the door. Slammed it, locked it, turned around, faced me.

His body vibrated like a wire pulled too tight.

Murder in his eyes.

While Alexa serenaded us.

Oh, no. Mamá! How would she survive my death? The pain would crush her, devastate her beyond words. And Papá! Tears filled my eyes, thinking of them, two of the people I loved most in the world. And, if I died now, never would I have a chance for a life with Manuel. At the thought, my heart wobbled like an object about to fall off a shelf.

I decided that if I made it through this, I'd convince my family about him, about us. It might take me some time, months, a year, or more, but it would be done. In my fantasies, I imagined them giving us permission without us having to ask.

"I shouldn't have said all that to you." Liam sounded surer of himself, apparently recuperated from his partial breakdown.

I stiffened, becoming a frozen image rendition of myself.

"You . . . you said nothing, Liam." The tremor in my voice was obvious, even to me.

"Oh, ha ha." In an instant, his facial features contorted, and I saw what might have been the last face Mil, and maybe Babette, laid eyes on just before dying.

Well, no, I realized. Mil had most likely been poisoned, or at least been given medication that caused a bad interaction. Had it been the same for Babette? Had he killed her, too?

Had he stayed by Mil's side as life ebbed out of her, a river running dry?

And look at me now! Mind babbling on during possibly the last moments of my own life!

"You know now, right, Carli?" He spoke in the sing-song voice of a man whose sanity had just left him, giving way for its opposite, insanity, to take over.

"I did ..., urgh, for a measly $100,000!" Huge sobs wracked his body, the tears falling in fast-running streams down his face.

"Why? Why, why, why?! TELL ME!" His eyes, wide open, stayed on me.

He stood, rigid, hands fisted at his sides. His desperation encircled him like a thick fog.

I jumped when he yelled. Couldn't even hide it. He wasn't just losing it. He'd *already* lost it.

I stared at him, my mind blank.

"What am I going to do now?" He asked, plaintive, like a young child who hadn't gotten his way, gazing around the room as if looking for something. But for what? A murder weapon?

Would my life end to the relaxing sounds of Enya and her ilk?

Instinct prompted me to say something; something kind.

I found my voice. Calm came over me. My usual when faced with true danger.

"Liam, it's okay. Whatever happened, I know you didn't mean it."

Lame. Weak. But I needed to say *something*. Anything.

The maniacal laugh of a horror movie clown erupted from him, his face changing as rapidly as landscapes seen through a speeding train window. I stared, entranced and terrified, fear gripping me as it never had.

My emotions changed as fast as the expressions on his face, and no longer calm, my whole body trembled. Though I felt no fear. Not really. The part of my brain that wanted to survive took over.

"Let me help you!" I exclaimed, but calmly, as if I were offering to help him clean up his house after a dinner party.

"Help me? *You* want to *help* me? You! Someone who hangs out with cops!" That lunatic clown laugh again.

I stood, transfixed, hoping the recording apps would pick up everything. Some of it, most of it?

"ALEXA! RAISE VOLUME!" He yelled, as if he'd overheard my thought.

A loud exclamation came from somewhere. But from where? I realized it had come from me.

"What, did I scare you, Carli?" He asked, sauntering toward me.

"I just don't want anyone to know what I'm about to say." He sounded as if he were whispering, what with the louder music.

He leaned in, voice conspiratorial, like we were co-conspirators, not predator and prey. My heart did somersaults so certain was I that he realized I'd turned on my recording apps.

Alexa moved on to Sting. Why was *Every Breath you Take* on a New Age song list?

Because he's about to snuff the breath out of you, came the thought.

I hiccupped a cry.

He was right in front of me now.

"Let's go," he said, grabbing my arm.

"Ow!" He'd grabbed my wrist tight and bent it.

"You'll be FINE."

Was that knocking coming from downstairs?

"Liam, no!" I tried to stop him. But he proved too strong for me. He pulled me behind him, like a boy pulling a red wagon full of rocks, eyes intent on his destination. Which turned out to be a door I hadn't paid attention to until now, in the far-left corner of the enormous room.

He swung it open and shoved me inside. I landed on the ground in a small walk-in closet. Despite everything, I noticed that shelves filled with shoes, handbags, and hats lined all three walls.

It smelled closed in and of the streets of San Miguel and Mil's sweat on the shoes.

"Liam, please!"

Fear overwhelmed my senses now, and it took me a moment to notice pain in my ankle. I'd landed on it wrong.

I could tell it was twisted, but not broken; no more pain than when I sometimes twisted it when wearing stilettos on our cobblestoned sidewalks—never a good idea. But a girl had to look good, you know?

"Who's at the door, huh, Carlota?" When he saw my look of surprise at the name, he added. "Yes, I know your full name." His voice came out in a threatening whisper, his breath hot and rank, filling the confined space, and mixing with the smell of the shoes.

"So. How do you want to go?" He asked.

Go? *Go where?* Wondered my befuddled mind.

"WELL?"

"Go where?" I stammered.

My gaze flicked to my tablet on the ground and out of reach, hoping it was still recording. I heard my phone ring again, from where I'd dropped it just outside the door—the third call since he'd pushed me into the closet.

He laughed again, a horrific sound.

"Not where. HOW!"

How?

Wait . . .

He wanted me to choose how I would die . . .

Chapter 30

O ne part of my mind thought it interesting that I could choose how I'd die. How many people got to make that choice?

Yet ... the hairs on my neck and arms stood at attention. I shoved my hands into my armpits and realized that my whole body was shaking. Breathing became difficult.

Fear.

The likes of which I'd never known, not even during that bad time in New York, its metallic taste filling my mouth and making me tremble.

"Liam, did you kill your moth ... Mil?"

There. I'd asked the question.

My heart pounded so loudly I feared he might hear it. His face remained agonized but inscrutable, and in that silence, I analyzed his every possible answer.

He stood over me, his back to the closed closet door. He seemed to think over my question while he stared at me. I couldn't hold his gaze. I looked down at the ground, noticing things in the closet out of my peripheral vision.

He allowed himself to fall to his knees, a marionette whose puppet master had let go of the strings for the legs.

Only then did he answer me.

"Kill her? No," he stammered, his voice cracking. "I just helped her along to her eventual destination." Liam's eyes were cold, unyielding. "I gave her a bit more than needed of something she took anyway. Or should have taken, every day. Prescribed, but often ignored by her. That warfarin stuff."

Unable to look away from him despite the horror of his words, I tried to understand what he was saying. He hadn't said what he'd said. Had he?

"Can't blame her," he muttered, looking away, his voice breaking. "I don't like taking mine either."

He puffed out a sigh, sounding as if he were trying not to cry.

His words hung in the air before landing in my consciousness, like a kite fluttering slowly to the ground after the wind suddenly dies. His twisted confession sent a chill down my spine. This wasn't the Liam I'd thought him to be. No loving son here ...

He continued. "She was old. She was selfish!" He harrumphed. "She wouldn't *help* me. A measly $100,000," he whined, a petulant child.

Our eyes locked in the awful knowledge of what he'd done for so little.

"But how? I mean ... why $100,000?"

Even in here, the sound of banging reached us from downstairs. Pounding. Then, a crash. Someone, or many *someones* downstairs intent on coming into the house, was my guess. My heart throbbed, mirroring the pandemonium. Liam's eyes widened, a realization dawning in them. The police ...

We sat on the floor of the closet, suspended in time, each still staring into the other's anguished eyes. Each trying to read the other's next move. Knowing help was so close flooded me with relief. And more anxiety. What would he do now, knowing he had nothing to lose?

He replied. "*How?* How else?"

What did that mean? He looked over his shoulder as if trying to see outside the closet door and into the rest of the house.

"And Babette?" I asked in a whisper, holding my breath.

This deep into the situation, why not get the whole truth from him?

"Babette?" He asked, looking as though he were scraping his memory for who she might be.

"Well, you see, Babette is a nosy body. *That's* what happened to Babette."

"Nosy?" I dared ask.

"She came in while I was working on getting rid of the evidence, that's what!" He huffed and puffed, the bad wolf trying to blow the house down. "She shouldn't have done that. OKAY? SHE SHOULD HAVE MINDED HER OWN BUSINESS!"

All I could do was stare.

"LIKE YOU, CARLI! LIKE YOU!"

"No, Liam. I didn't ..."

"YES! YOU'VE BEEN NOSING AROUND TRYING TO FIGURE IT ALL OUT!"

His face contorted, a mask of rage like I'd never seen. His words, a garbled mess in my ears. Fear thundered in me overshadowing everything else.

How had it come to this? Still down on his knees, he leaned toward me.

And put his hands around my throat.

And squeezed.

I shouldn't have held my breath so much.

Now I'd run out of air before I might have, otherwise. Before rescue arrived. With it just outside the door. Seconds too late ...

Sting sang on. *Every breath you take, every move you make, every bond you break, every step you take ...*

The harder I tried to pry his hands off my neck, the harder he squeezed. My head filled with pounding, the blood about to burst from my veins.

A scream came from inside my head; *HIT HIM IN THE YOU-KNOW-WHATS!* But just trying to breathe took all my energy.

Gurgling sounds filled our space. Mine.

From somewhere, I found enough strength to let go of his hands long enough to insert my arms between his, push outward to loosen his grip on me. It caused him to lose his balance and fall back against the closet door. Something cracked. Would the door give in and break? I hoped the police would hear it, but with the music so loud, they probably wouldn't.

I managed to stand by grabbing onto shelves on both sides of me and pulling myself up enough to deliver a good kick. Got him with my booted foot right in his you-know-whats. He squealed, something that sounded between a baby's wail and a guttural, primordial scream, a man reacting to extreme pain.

Muffled yelling reached us. "LIAM JONES! Police!"

I couldn't find the strength or the breath to respond to them.

My eyes never left Liam, though. He seemed to have given up. curled on the floor in the fetal position, his hands at his crotch, moaning.

"LIAM JONES! Police!"

The voice sounded much closer. I realized whose voice it was. I went to climb over Liam to open the door, but he grabbed my ankle, which caused me to fall to the floor once more.

"Oh, no, *oh* no." He grumbled. "You're not going ... nowhere, Carli!" The words came out strangled, as if someone had their hands around *his* throat.

"Antonio! In here!" I croaked, not loud enough for him to hear with all the shoes providing insulation while the music played on in the bedroom.

A lot of yelling found its way to the interior of my prison. The sound of boots on the wooden stairs. And more yelling.

"CARLI! LIAM JONES!" Antonio.

Other voices resounded from different parts of the house. "*POLICIA*!"

Liam stirred, so to keep him down, I grabbed a wedge-heeled shoe from a shelf to my right and hit him on the head with all my might. Then, for good measure, I threw it at the door behind him. They'd heard that, surely? I didn't dare try to step over him again to open the door.

Surprise, shock, and pain elicited an anguished cry from him.

"Why, you ..." he said, his voice coming out in a whisper. He didn't get to finish before I hit him again, this time with a flat shoe. In the face. He screamed.

Two seconds later, the closet door burst open, and a rush of fresh air hit me like a wave. At the same time, a determined and flush-faced Antonio stormed in. I had never, *ever*, been so happy to see him. Ever.

Three other officers piled into the closet right behind him, their movements precise and practiced. They grabbed Liam, flipped him over on his stomach, and cuffed him. Efficiently and a bit brutally, I thought.

The sound of the metallic click of the handcuffs, the harsh breathing of the officers, the muted protests of Liam who was coming to, the shouting of police officers and the commotion seemed to fade, replaced by the intense pounding of my heart and the ragged sound of my own breathing.

The three officers who'd cuffed him dragged Liam into the bedroom, his body limp and defeated, his face a mask of shock and fear.

I drank in the fresher air from the open door, so grateful for it, but coughing and gasping nonetheless, every sensation amplified.

The distant sounds of other officers securing the area, the relief in Antonio's eyes as he kneeled in front of me—all of it surreal while being all too real. Somehow, it grounded me in this first moment after the terror of having almost been strangled to death. I continued to guzzle air as if it were a disappearing commodity.

Just before enveloping me in his arms, Antonio yelled out the closet door.

"MANUEL! *Aqui*!" In here. As if Manuel could see through walls to find us, as if he could tell where the *aqui* Antonio spoke of actually was.

I chuckled a bit despite my distress, so grateful for the ordinariness of hearing Antonio yelling at Manuel, and hearing Manuel out in the hall yelling back a frustrated "*¿DÓNDE?!*" at Antonio. Where. A typical exchange for them. One not explaining something very well to the other.

I clutched my throat, a torrent of emotions overwhelming me. Anger directed at Liam and his unfathomable choices. How could he, while professing to love her, end his own mother's life? This fury intertwined with a profound sadness for the path he'd taken. These feelings added to a sensory storm overwhelmed me: the sharp tang of my own fear, the well-worn scent of shoes, and the lingering mix of Antonio's citrusy aftershave mingled with sweat.

More anger for putting myself in this predicament, gratefulness I'd found the courage to kick him *there*, which had not only brought attention to us but had avoided me the same fate as Millicent and Babette.

Manuel rushed in and moved Antonio aside. He took over the job of wrapping his arms around me, and his warm embrace steadied me, comforted me, and calmed my trembling body. I buried my face in his shoulder, and noticed the salty taste of my tears, which had reached my lips.

I clung to the familiarity of Manuel's presence, my anchor in the world, the north I kept turning to despite the impossibility of a relationship with him.

We stayed there a while, me in his arms, both on our knees on the closet floor, a lot of commotion around Liam, and what sounded like at least a dozen cops talking and moving about around the bedroom.

The chaos of the rescue receded for me. Then Antonio came back into the closet to check on us.

"So," I managed. "Now you two get here?" I cleared my throat. "Where were you when I needed you?" I managed to say, voice raspy and with no oomph to it at all. "I mean, I had to save myself ..."

They stared at me in a way that gave me no idea at all what they were thinking.

CHAPTER 31

The next day, on my rooftop deck, glorious sunshine bathing us in its cleansing light, Antonio looked like someone only now coming to the realization of how dark the world was sometimes. You'd think he'd be used to it. But, no.

Antonio hid a soft heart behind that machismo persona of his. I only knew of it because of having spent all that time with him growing up.

He, Manuel, and I congregated around my coffee table, enjoying the sunshine despite our heavy mood. But, also, relief filled the surrounding air.

The thing was over.

Our circle had been restored to order.

On a more personal and immediate level, I could already feel my throat heal. And my ankle, which, thankfully, had only suffered a mild sprain.

• • • ● ● ● ● ● • • •

Manuel had taken me to my parents' as soon as Antonio had released me after taking my statement at the police station. My parents had hovered, gushed, put cold compresses on my neck, loved me with all their hearts, called in our family doctor, also a friend, who'd dropped everything to come immediately despite my protests.

He had declared me only in need of rest. I'd spent the night but had cajoled my father into taking me back to my house in town early this morning, before *Mamá* woke up and began to fuss over me.

Last night, unable to help myself, I'd gone back online to dig deeper into Liam Jones's affairs.

I scrolled beyond the first two pages, after which I'd given up when I first searched for him. It seemed like a lifetime ago, though it had only been a few days.

There, halfway down the third page of results, his name showed up in the preview text for a conservation branch of the City of Dallas. Ah, I thought, curious, staring at the link. Now intent as a cat on a mission to get the mouse it saw slip through a crack in the baseboard, I clicked on the link.

A page opened to details about a city council meeting where Liam Jones developer had been told he couldn't build a four-story condo building in Oak Cliff, not next to a park-slash-preserve. The residents of the area wouldn't have it.

No, it didn't matter how much he'd paid for the land; he should have checked with them first to be certain there would be no issues since the property he'd bought was in a conservation district.

Yes, they understood a city staff member had given him a verbal before the closing of the escrow. They were aware, but that person had been wrong to do so, and had since left for a position in Michigan. It seemed to them that a diligent developer would have checked deeper, gotten something in writing, they told him. They wouldn't budge, so Liam was suing them.

The article said nothing about how much the land had cost, but that was something I could figure out myself by visiting the recorder's office for that county; luckily, the U.S. government had such public records online nowadays, so looking it up involved only the time needed to search for the property. I found the address of the property in question in another article and accessed the recorder's office website.

Well, he'd paid a lot for it. And based on what I read, he'd planned two four-story L-shaped buildings, six units per floor. That meant twenty-four units per building, so a total of forty-eight units, but the city would only allow up to two stories in that area of the district, which allowed for only twenty-four units to be built. I knew little about property development, or how much a developer might profit from such a project, but knew enough about business to understand it would have hurt his bottom line a lot, if not turned it red. He'd only have been able to build half the units he'd planned on.

He'd been hurting. Since he couldn't deliver as promised, the investors had wanted their money back. Understandable.

He'd obviously already used a good chunk of the money to buy the land and selling it fast enough—even at a discount—to pay back the investors wasn't possible. It would take time.

So, based on what he'd told me yesterday, he'd turned to the one person who had large sums of money available immediately. His mother. But she'd turned him down ...

The story had become much clearer to me, but there had still been holes in it. Why had she turned him down, for instance?

And sitting around at my family home while my worried mother hovered wouldn't have brought me any answers.

Now on my beloved roof terrace with my two favorite cousins, these insights weighing on my mind, I wanted to know more. And Antonio had the answers.

I'd made Manuel and Antonio each their own French press carafe of coffee, and they'd brought me a vente matcha tea. Dap, lying on the warm stone floor somewhat away from us, occupied himself with licking his paws like someone proud of a job well done.

The typical street noises of Centro reached us. People calling to one another, the ringing bells of a church or other some distance away—there seemed to always be an event worth tolling a bell for somewhere in town—car horns, children laughing, even a daytime mariachi band.

I gazed toward the pink wedding-cake-like pinnacles and spires of the Parroquia four blocks away, whose own bells were quiet for now. A beautiful view that always inspired me.

My voice raspy, I mused "I just can't believe he did that to his own mother. And then, to commit a *second* murder?" I sighed. "The drugs, I guess ..."

"Not to mention, he nearly got you, Carlita," said Manuel, his voice gentle, gazing at his coffee cup, which he turned round and round in his hands, sitting a little hunched over.

My heart swelled seeing him like this, looking so worried, even now, when it was all over.

Antonio sat back in his chair, legs spread out ahead of him, hands on his thighs. He nodded his head, lips pursed, his eyes big on me, no doubt recalling what had to have been my beet-red face when he found me and Liam on the floor of the closet.

I took a sip of matcha and winced. The pain swallowing brought reminded me of Liam's hands squeezing my throat with all their might, less than eighteen hours ago.

"I mean, he's not a normal criminal, right?" I asked.

Antonio dipped his head to his right and raised his eyebrows at me before answering.

"Few people are *real* criminals, Carli. The cartel, the mafias of the world, yes, but not the Liams. He was stuck in a bind, got scared, got caught, and repeated the process. He won't like prison here ..."

"I can imagine." And I could, but also, I couldn't. No thinking about it. He'd committed the crimes.

"Again, I'm ever so thankful you found me, *muchos gracias, primos, muchos muchos gracias.*" Thank you so very much, my cousins. Tears came to my eyes.

· · · ● ● · ● ● · · ·

Just an hour before they'd found me in the closet with Liam, the dealer he'd used for crack when in San Miguel—a habit he'd resumed when his troubles had started—had been arrested in an unrelated raid and forced to name his customers. Liam had been one of them. Call it cop's instinct, Antonio understood immediately he had to find Liam.

Just after he'd sent officers to Liam's house, he'd opened his email and saw mine, and blanched at what I'd done, at me more or less breaking into a house and leaving it with evidence. He then recalled how curious and persistent I could be when wanting to know something. That's when he'd started calling me.

When he couldn't reach me, after dialing my number over and over, he got suspicious and called the shop. Esme told him I'd be out until late afternoon, but that she didn't know where I'd gone. Again, on instinct, and thinking of me, he decided to go to Mil's, too, right on the heels of the officers he'd sent. On his way there, he called Manuel at the restaurant—who had ripped off his apron and rushed over, too.

They said nothing to my repeated thank yous. They both saw me as having been foolish. But, also knowing how stubborn I could be, they realized how useless any reminder of the danger my foolishness put me in would be.

Finally, Antonio repeated Liam's confession to Manuel and me.

After they'd arrested him and gotten him into an interrogation room, the complete story had tumbled out of him, but not until after Antonio had played back a portion of my recordings to him. Recordings that turned out to be clear enough, and where one sounded muffled, the other often picked up.

Liam broke down, cried hard for several minutes before he talked. Then, in spurts, he'd confessed everything to Antonio and another detective.

"I just want to die!" He'd said to Antonio.

Unfortunately for him, Mexico didn't have the death penalty, so he'd suffer the consequences of his actions for many years to come—in a most brutal prison.

"The whole thing started back in Dallas with a problem on his latest project there." Said Antonio.

CHAPTER 32

I nodded because I already knew that. He continued the story and I waited eagerly for him to give me the pieces I was missing.

"He said he wasn't sure what he'd do once he got here, but brought all his prescription drugs from home, including warfarin. Mil was on it too, so he figured her taking a bunch of it would seem she'd done herself in or taken too much by mistake."

Manuel and I glanced at one another. Exactly what I'd said early on; he'd poisoned her in an overdose way. And to think ... what if I'd accepted his offer of pot pie yesterday and he'd added drugs to that, too? I cringed at the thought.

Antonio stopped so he could pour himself a second cup of coffee, and the rich aroma of fresh brew reached me from all the way across the coffee table. He added sugar to it, the clink of his spoon as he stirred filling the silence. He took a sip, and added more sugar. I rolled my eyes. The man had the sweet tooth of a ten-year-old.

He continued.

"So, before he did anything, he asked Mil for the money to bail him out. She said no. Said she told him it was time for him to stand on his own two feet, that his whole life she'd bailed him out, and he'd never had an opportunity to test what he could do in life."

"I've seen some ugly things, and you have, too," said Manuel, looking at Antonio. "But, to kill your own mother who never did anything bad to you ...," he added, gazing off into the distance in dismay.

Antonio was nodding his head as Manuel spoke. He added to it. "Not the first time. And not the last ..."

"Anyway, Liam said she told him, *I'll be dead in a few years, and you'll have plenty of money to retire on, Liam. Meanwhile, see what you can do about restoring your own faith in yourself. I shouldn't have spoiled you like I did. Here you are, a sixty-year-old man asking his mother for money.*

"So, he felt he had no choice. The Dallas vultures wouldn't let him off the hook. They'd take his project from him. He said he saw it as his signature project, the one to retire on with admiration from other builders."

He stopped to take another sip of coffee. I looked around my beautiful terrace, at the vibrant colors of the blooming bougainvillea, gardenias, and honeysuckle, appreciating the whole even more after yesterday's trauma. But despite that and the warmth of the morning sun, I shivered, recalling those events. And wondered ... how could a son betray his own mother like that? How?

Manuel, as if sensing my distress, reached over and patted my shoulder. Antonio looked at us like he wondered how we did that, read one another's mind, as we seemed to do so often.

"I guess some people get handed too many lemons," Manuel said.

"Or take too many drugs." I grumbled.

"That, too," said Antonio.

"But why did he kill Babette? What did she have to do with all this?"

Liam hadn't told me, only that she hadn't minded her own business. And the question had been eating at me all night.

Antonio shook his head a few times before answering me.

"The day you saw her at Mil's house, she'd used the key Mil gave her, when no one answered the door. They helped one another out and she was checking on her. They were good friends according to some people, though how true that is, I don't know."

He stopped once again to take a sip of coffee.

Manuel and I said nothing, just looked at Antonio, me sending him vibes to hurry. Manuel, even more impatient than me when it came to our cousin, tapped his fingers on the armrest of his chair, which told me that Antonio's habit of dragging stories out and adding unnecessary details was getting to him.

"And then?" he pressed, urging Antonio to continue.

"Liam, paranoid because of the crack cocaine he'd been snorting since early in the morning, was crushing warfarin tablets into the sink before sending them down the drain. He'd decided that it would look suspicious, having those around since he knew it was what he gave his mother. Babette startled him when she called to him from the doorway to the kitchen. He thought she could see into the sink from across the room."

He sighed, shaking his head at Liam's actions, conveying that he saw it as a dumb move.

"Well, paranoia *does* things like that to a man," said Manuel.

"*Sí*. Anyway, she sat herself down and asked after Mil, and he realized she hadn't heard yet. So, after a few minutes of conversation, he told her. Maybe she saw nothing or wouldn't understand if she did, he reasoned. But she came toward him to hug him, to say sorry about Mil. Says his blood pressure rose through the roof, sure she'd now see what he was doing and realize what it meant."

I stared, mesmerized at how such a small innocent, kind gesture had been her undoing. Antonio continued.

"He decided to kill her, too."

He paused to let us absorb the gruesome truth of that.

"Right there and then, while she was in front of him. The stupidity of some people." His face showed his disdain over that.

"He said because he wasn't going to jail in Mexico. And he wasn't going to have people know what he did to his own mother. The fool thought he could get his inheritance, go back to Dallas, and settle things there."

Anger rose in me. Babette had gone to Mil's house with only offering help to her friend in mind, yet it had gotten her killed. Sometimes, the unfairness of life just ...

We all remained silent, contemplating Liam's evil plan, while dogs barking back and forth from various roofs reached us.

"Would it have worked if he hadn't gotten so paranoid?" I asked.

Antonio toggled his head, a bit like a bobble head, a few times before answering.

"I don't think so. She wasn't depressed, based on everyone we talked to. Who would go to a concert, have fun at a party, then go home and take a whole bottle of warfarin? Yes, people can seem normal before they kill themselves, but not acting very happy like her."

"How many did she take?" I corrected myself. "I mean, how many did he give her?"

"No way to know for sure. The coroner can tell it was too many because of all the internal bleeding. That's how they figured it out, apparently. Even her brain was bleeding. She had bruises all over too, from the bleeding. They just know that it takes fifteen to thirty pills to kill someone."

"But how did he give it to her?" I asked.

"Oh, and what about that anti-depressant from Bill? It didn't do anything?" I added.

I'd nearly forgotten that Denise had put an anti-depressant into a glass of wine intended for her own husband—because he too often didn't take it voluntarily—but that Mil had drunk the wine instead.

"Nope. What Mil got from Denise wasn't enough. It can happen, yes, but not likely that the one tablet of Elavil on top of the Parnate she already took, another thing the coroner discovered in her, would have killed her." His hands moved animatedly as he recounted this to his captive audience, in his full element, describing a crime after it had been solved.

"But there's no doubt, this much warfarin is lethal, regardless of any reaction to anti-depressants. And the warfarin was on purpose, so Liam wins as the killer."

He shrugged as if what he said was obvious and stared into his coffee.

I felt relieved for Denise.

He went on. "Anyway, he cooked dinner for his mother and himself while she was at the concert and party. She'd promised to eat with him once she got home. He crushed the tablets into mashed potatoes and added a spicy *salsa verde* on top to mask any taste, except I found out there's no taste. But Liam didn't know that." He harrumphed, as if appalled with Liam for not learning that if he was going to kill someone with it.

I recalled her saying something at the party about waiting to eat with her son once she got home, that he'd surprised her by arriving in town that afternoon.

"What is that stuff, anyway? What does it do? How come they were both on it?" I asked.

"It controls a heart issue, something pretty common. If you have it, it causes small blood clots to form and go to the brain, which can give you an aneurysm. That drug stops it."

"And ... what, Liam had it because Mil had it," said Manuel, more statement than question.

Antonio pointed a finger back at Manuel, nodding in agreement. "Yes. The coroner told me it can run in families. But you can have it even if no one in your family does."

We all sat silent for a moment. I gazed at Dap, whose life seemed so much simpler than mine. A part of me wanted to be taken care of in the way I took care of him. I glanced at Manuel, who, impatient now, addressed Antonio.

"Babette?" He looked at Antonio with raised eyebrows.

"Sí, getting to that, *vato*."

Manuel and I exchanged a look, me rolling my eyes, discreetly, so our cousin wouldn't notice.

Antonio loved the drama of being in charge of telling a good story, and Manuel was too impatient to not try to rush him along, which never worked. He'd just slow down and give even more details. I wanted to get to the end, to know everything.

"So, anyway, he decided on the spot to load up Babette with oxycontin because he thought it would look suspicious if she died of a warfarin overdose too."

I sat up straight, surprised, and curious. "Oxycontin? That strong pain killer? The one in the news? How did he get that?"

"Said he got a prescription for it two years ago for back pain, but he didn't take it then because of his addiction issue. He put up with the pain instead. I guess he was still level-headed then. Things just got too much for him with the money I guess " He shrugged.

"Wow ... that's ... how sad." I said.

Manuel nodded his head, gazing at the table in front of him like it held the story instead of it coming from Antonio.

"Yes, but don't feel too sorry. He *did* kill his own mother." Said Antonio the cop.

"He decided to bring the oxycontin, too, when he came down here, not really knowing why, he said."

"He brought it with him from Dallas?"

This surprised me.

"Why not?" asked Antonio. "It's legal if you have a prescription. Nobody really checks the expiration date. And anyway, even if the prescription bottle says it expired say, six months ago, doesn't mean someone can't still have them."

I nodded my head. That made sense.

Manuel spoke. "These guys. How do they think that stuff will make their lives better, I don't understand it."

"No se, vato. No se," said Antonio, his voice singsong.

"Anyway, his mind was a mess."

"How much oxycontin did he give her?" I asked, always curious about such things.

"Ah, *no se*. Enough to kill her. They can't tell for sure how many pills a person took, only that it was in their system, and that it was too much."

I took a deep breath, took a sip of matcha, and hoped Antonio would get to the end of the story before *comida*—four hours from now.

Manuel shifted in his chair and looked off toward the Parroquia whose turn it seemed had now come to toll her bells.

We all waited until it stopped, then Manuel and I turned to Antonio.

Perhaps, for once, noticing our impatience, he continued.

"Anyway, he offered her coffee and a bowl of soup the maid had cooked the day before. She accepted. He excused himself, went to his bedroom, crushed a couple dozen tablets and dumped them into a handkerchief, then returned to the kitchen. Where he put it all into Babette's soup. And, of course, her friend found her the next day ..."

I sighed, deep and long. Manuel shifted, raised his arms above his head and stretched.

We sat, silent, nothing more to be said. Dap got up on all fours, meowed once, loudly, and ran inside. What did he mean by it? I wondered briefly. His soft, mysterious glance lingered in my mind. Sometimes I understood him perfectly, other times, not at all.

Manuel glanced at my fleeing cat, then at me, a questioning look in his eyes, as if I were responsible for his abrupt departure.

"What? I didn't do anything." Sometimes I wondered if Manuel, who spoiled his own cat rotten, thought I was abusing Dap.

Antonio, looking from me to Manuel and back again, chuckled. With no cat of his own, he just couldn't understand the differences in cat parenting.

The Parroquia bells tolled yet again. I took the last sip of my matcha. Antonio shook the glass French press, as if that would miraculously add more coffee to it. I could see the grounds shifting and settling at the bottom. Manuel, his hands now linked behind his head, gazed into the distance.

The good part was that it was over. We could rest again, not worry someone else in our circle would be murdered at any moment.

At least, one might hope that wouldn't happen.

"I guess I should take some sort of self-defense class, you know. Just in case?"

Had I been able to defend myself better yesterday, I might not have ended up with Liam's hands around my throat, doing his best to squeeze the life out of me.

I'd been looking into my empty cup as I said it, so it took a moment for me to realize that my cousins seemed unusually quiet.

I looked up to see them both skewering me with intense looks.

"What?" I asked, bemused.

EPILOGUE

T wo days later, on a beautiful fall day, the air was crisp, and the sun shone soft and bright in an azure sky dotted with puffy white clouds. The promise of a perfect day.

I strolled to my shop, each step filled with a lightness that mirrored my cheerful heart, and I floated along the sidewalks as if on a cloud, embracing the world around me.

I could breathe freely.

Of course, San Miguel reeled with the news of the murders. Conspiracy stories abounded; rumors flew off the charts, even for this town. But that was the way here. One accepted it. Or left One participated. Or not.

There would be a memorial service, or rather, a celebration of life for Mil, which is what many people in her circle said she'd wanted. No one would ask her son what he thought her wishes might have been.

And Babette's two children and their families had arrived in town last night. I didn't know what they had in mind yet, but she'd been living in San Miguel for several years, so surely there would be a memorial service for her, too.

As a bonus, Luna was back in town, and we'd made plans to go out to dinner the next night. She always cheered me beyond reason.

Arriving in the courtyard at my shop, I noticed Lisa at the coffee cart. She waved and said she'd see me in a minute. My heart sank. No part of me wanted to go over all the gruesome details of the last week. Especially not with the biggest gossip in town. But, business, you know?

Ten minutes later, she entered the shop, her perfume, as usual, overbearing.

"Carli, how are you, eh?" Anticipation of the gossip she hoped would come from me lit up her face like a second sun.

"I'm well, Lisa. You?"

"Oh, you know, after all this stuff, phew." She shook her head back and forth, looking at me like one waiting in anticipation for goodies to drop out of a gum ball machine.

"That's good."

"So. What happened? How did you figure it out about Liam?"

"I ... didn't. As you heard, I'm sure, he confessed. I just happened to be there, nothing else." I knew she knew this much because a reporter had somehow found out and said so in the article he'd written for the largest expat newspaper, so I could say it.

I gave her the smile I reserved for customers best kept at bay because otherwise, they'd eat up the whole day.

"Are you looking for something specific? Dinner party dress, or something more casual?" I asked, pretending we didn't both know she needed nothing, that she'd come to get the inside story to spread around as if she had been there herself.

Her smile expanded slowly, a knowing in her eyes. "Well, now, Carli, I wondered how it all happened, you know? I mean, this doesn't happen every day in our town, eh. We have a right to understand these things. So we can prevent them in the future. Don't you agree?"

She stood, rigid, straight, a woman pretending to herself to be doing her civic duty.

I looked at her, this woman who somehow always managed to get to me with her insatiable appetite for gossip. No way was she getting any fuel from me to spread on the fires she lit with her big mouth. Only my closest allies would know what happened to me at Mil's house.

"That's true," I said. At which she perked up. Until I continued. "Why not go pay Antonio a visit, he's always up for helping our community stay safe."

Her left eye twitched up a notch, but when she was about to speak, the cheerful tinkle of the door windchime sounded as the door opened, and Sofia walked in.

"So, so sorry, *lo siento*, Carli! My alarm didn't go off!"

I'd never been this happy to see her arrive late, this being perfect timing for the moment at hand.

"That's okay, Sofia. Please help Lisa if she needs it. I need to go into my office and take care of some bills."

"Have fun browsing, Lisa!" And at that, I walked to the back of the store toward my office, giving her a casual wave over my shoulder with just my fingers, before she could say anything else, happy to have made my escape.

Just then, my cell phone rang. I looked at the display. Amy!

I smiled, knowing at some point I'd tell *her* the whole story. But only in person. Not over the phone. Perhaps she'd come to dinner with Luna and me. We'd go to Manuel's Eatery and let him spoil us with morsels he seemed to magically create in that kitchen of his.

Yes, *todo está bien con mi mundo*, I thought. All is well with my world.

My bio-father's handsome face came to mind, and warmth enveloped me. My parents' smiling faces and their love for me added to my happiness. Manuel, Antonio, Luna, Amy, all my favorite people.

Despite the gossip, despite the small troubles, and the big ones that came along occasionally, I couldn't have been happier about being here in my favorite place.

Of course, this, like everything, could change.

A growing town meant more people.

More people meant more bad seeds among them. Not to mention the ones that already hid among us and could sprout at any time.

But on this day, at least, yes, all *was* well.

Carli wants for everything to remain well in her world, sure. But, you know, life (and mayhem) happens ...

Cozy up with more Carli Cano mysteries—Just two quick clicks, and voilà – you're diving into your next amazing read at your favorite online bookstore!

When Music Meets Murder (Book 1)

When Mayhem Means Murder (Book 2)

Mayhem No More (Book 3)

Stitched in Deceit (The Prequel That Started It All!)

Got a print copy and eager to find all the links to the next books in one handy spot? Just head over to Carli's corner on my website – you'll find everything you need right there!

https://maryselaflamme.com/carli-cano-mystery-series

LOVED THE BOOK? PLEASE BE A HERO IN MY STORY!

I f you had fun with Carli and crew, the best way to support my work is by leaving a quick review!

Seriously—reviews are rocket fuel for indie authors like me. We don't survive without them.

I don't have the big bucks needed to plaster Times Square with ads, but I *can* reach more readers with your help.
Just a few words—no sonnets required (though I'd totally frame one if you wrote it).

Here's the direct link to leave your review:
https://maryselaflamme.com/review/

Your words help more than you know—and keeps future books coming.

Thank you from me, Carli, Manuel, Antonio, Luna ... and the rest of the fictional gang. You really are the cherry on top.

THE AUTHOR

Meet Maryse Laflamme—the *matcha-sipping, mystery-spinning, AI-taming (for everything but writing books because it sucks at that), bone-broth-brewing badass* who turned a death sentence into a launchpad. At 71, she's living proof that reinvention has no age limit — from crafting compelling fiction in whatever corner of the world the wind last tossed her, to building an author empire powered by no-bloat blueprints and digital smarts.

She writes like she's talking to her sharpest, sassiest friend—and helps writers skip the overwhelm and actually finish their damn books. When she's not demystifying AI for new authors, she's spinning worldly mysteries with grit, glamour, and just enough danger to keep you up at night. Her voice? Irreverent, insightful, and infused with wisdom earned from a life well-traveled—and almost lost.

She made an incurable cancer her bitch, and came back armed with a pen, a plan, a story to tell, a vision to share, and zero patience for small talk or safe choices.

Cozy up with more Carli Cano mysteries. Just two quick clicks, and voilà—you're diving into your next amazing read at your favorite online bookstore!

When Music Meets Murder (Book 1)

When Mayhem Means Murder (Book 2)

Mayhem No More (Book 3)

Stitched in Deceit (The Prequel That Started It All!)

Got a print copy and eager to find all the links to the next books in one handy spot? Just head over to Carli's corner on my website—you'll find everything you need right there! https://maryselaflamme.com/carli-cano-mystery-series

Dive Deeper into Maryse Laflamme's World!

Got questions, comments, or your own mini mystery to share? Reach out through the contact form on her website. She's a reply wizard, unless you're sending Spam—then expect to be catapulted to the farthest reaches of the Universe!

Stalk—uh, no, *follow* her online!

Here's where you can catch all her latest musings and clues:

Website: MaryseLaflamme.com

Facebook: Maryse Laflamme Writer

Instagram: @maryselaflammewriter

CARLI CANO MYSTERY SERIES BOOK 2 PREVIEW

WHEN MAYHEM MEANS MURDER—PROLOGUE

M y cell phone broke out in a dance from the front pouch of my Coach handbag. The metallic zipper brushed against my fingers as I reached in to grab it.

But it was a call I could have done without.

I frowned when I saw the name on the caller ID.

"Hola, Adele," I greeted her, trying to sound upbeat, hearing the muffled murmur of her nearby television.

"Carli!" she exclaimed, the urgency in her voice palpable.

"Wh ... what?!" I asked, my heart drumming against my chest, echoing the loud raindrops that began to tap against my window.

"He's gone!"

"Gone wh ... " But realization struck, the coldness settling in my stomach like a chunk of ice. An intense tremor ran down my spine, electrifying me.

"No! No, no, no!" Shock rippled through me.

"How?" I managed, fingers trembling, the phone's cool screen pressing against my cheek.

"Not sure. He was found bleeding ... so much blood ... on the ground ..."

The weight of her words pressed down on me, thickening the air in the room, while Dapper circled my legs, meowing.

My thoughts raced, the distant barks of a neighbor's roof dog distracting me.

"Carli?" Adele's voice cut through, sharper than the piercing wail of a nearby siren, probably on its way to the scene.

"¿Mande? I don't know what to say." I responded, momentarily disoriented, the sirens becoming a distant murmur.

A pause. The heavy beat of my heart filled the silence.

Then, "Someone said there's a chance he was going ..." Her voice faded away as if she was losing reception.

"Going to what?" I nearly yelled, not wanting to lose the connection, wondering if she'd been about to say what I thought she'd say. The room seemed to tilt, the faint hum of the ceiling fan above me growing more pronounced.

The gravity of the situation hit me. What tangled webs we weave.

I got a dial tone. She was gone.

I had to know more. Hanging up, desperate for answers, I dialed Antonio. No answer the first time, or the second. The silence between the rings felt suffocating.

On the third try, his exasperated voice came through. "Carlota! I'm in the middle of this!"

I bristled at his use of my birth name, the dim glow of a nearby streetlight filtering through my sheer curtains.

"Someone I know might be involved in this mess, Antonio!"

"And I'm here with my team trying to get to the bottom of it. You blowing up my phone is not helping."

He hung up on me.

But this happened much later. First came everything that led to it ...

Gain Access to When Mayhem Means Murder, Book 2 of the Carli Cano Mystery Series

https://amzn.to/42er9Ef

www.ingramcontent.com/pod-product-compliance
Lightning Source LLC
Chambersburg PA
CBHW020358210626
46816CB00006BB/2028